football seasons

mick bower

For Lucy

Pulp Books is an imprint of Pulp Faction
PO Box 12171, London N19 3HB.
First published by Pulp Books, 1998.
All rights reserved.

A CIP record for this book is available
from the British Library.
ISBN 1901072061

football seasons

mick bower

2nd May 1981

Walsall (h)

May 2nd 81. For some of us, it's right up there. 1066, 1492, 1914, 1966, May 2nd 1981.

I probably woke up about half nine, but it's hard to say. All night I'd been mulling it over, thinking the unthinkable. The doomsday scenario. Another hour of soul searching, then I dragged myself out of bed. D-Day had started. The pressure was on. You could taste it in the air, the teenage cocktail of anticipation and dread. Sixteen is a tough age for anyone. For a Sheff United fan ... let's just say it's pretty fucking hard.

It looked like it was going to be a nice day, out. Through the window I could see the sun shining off the cars on the motorway. You can see our house from the M1; it's one of the terraces on the Rotherham side of the Tinsley viaduct, but it is in Sheffield. Rotherham might be only a few hundred yards away, but I'm a Sheffield lad. A city boy.

I took a bit longer than usual to get ready. Big game; had to look the part. At the time dressing up for games hadn't really caught on, only a few of the top lads were into it. I thought it was a waste of money, all them designer labels, but I could see the reasons behind it. Always important to make the right impression. I was a bit of a plastic skinhead. I was well into the music, The Specials and all that, and everybody had loved Sham. My mate Gary was a proper bonehead. He was more into the punk side of it. I'd borrowed loads of his albums to tape, some of it was really good. I'd been to see the Angelic Upstarts with him a few weeks before. That'd been fucking mental—best gig I'd ever been to.

I had a crew-cut. I didn't think the blokes at United would appreciate a crop. Anyway, there were loads of places in town where you couldn't get in if you were a bonehead. I couldn't see the point in it. My match day clothes were pretty standard, but I thought I looked the business. Short sleeved, burgundy Lonsdale, Levi's and Doc shoes. Whenever I was ready to go out, I'd always look at myself in the mirror for a bit. Acting hard or sexy; whichever was appropriate for the place I was heading off to. I'm sure everybody does it, but it's one of those things you don't talk about. Same as wanking or watching the news.

No question about the image I was aiming for that day. Paul Andrews—top Blade. Paul Andrews—hard bastard. Paul Andrews—loyal Unitedite.

—Come on then you Brummie cunt …
—UNITED, UNITED …
—What ya come ere for? Let's ave it dickhead.
The business.

Paul Andrews, loyal Blade, went downstairs for his breakfast. When I was halfway through my cornflakes my dad, Brian Andrews, know-nothing bag of shit, walked in. I was waiting for it.

—Off to t'Lane are tha?

—Aye.

—Mek most on it, cos they wain't be playin big teams like Walsall forra bit. It'll be t'likes o Crewe an Rochdale next year.

I ignored him. He loved it; wallowing in failure. That's all him and his cronies up at the club ever did. Sit around and talk about work and how grim everything was. Laugh a minute stuff.

—If they keep goin down at this rate, I might start goin again. I'll be able to tek dog out o'er t'playin fields an watch em on a Sunday mornin.

—Bollocks.

—Tha what?

My mam came in from the kitchen to call break. She was always telling me to ignore the old man. She had for years. Everybody did. Everybody except his mates at the club. They were all the same as him: school to steelworks and stayed there. No ambition past a few pints a night. Anyone who didn't want the same was a 'daft cunt'. If United lost they'd all laugh about it; same as if they won. I hated them.

No way was I going to end up like that. I had a chance to be someone. This gave our old man status at the club.

7

Ever since I'd played for Sheffield boys he'd been, 'Brian, whose lad's a good footballer'. Since I'd signed apprentice forms, he'd become, 'Brian, whose lad's wi t'Blades'. He couldn't see that they all wanted me to fail and end up like them, so they could all have a laugh. If he hadn't been taking the credit, he would too.

—I were only avin a joke. It's im who started comin it.

—Just leave im Brian, will ya?

Our old man wasn't in the mood for a row with my mam. Probably because he always lost. Instead he asserted his authority by staring at me, then changing the transistor from Radio One to Radio Sheffield. Pretty fucking hard, eh? As usual, a phone-in was on; wads of indignant South Yorkshire folk saying 'disgusting' and 'disgraceful'. Our old man's natural habitat. Definitely time for a sharp exit.

Even on a sunny day, Tinsley looks like a shithole. It's not a bad area, it just looks it. The houses have all been up yonks and have had decades of whatever the surrounding works pump out to put up with. Apart from the grime, a lot of people are put off by the large local Asian population. I'd never had any bother with them. Grew up with them, went to school with them, full works. They did their own thing. Kept themselves to themselves, but if we ever had hassle with a mob from another area, they'd always turn out and stand with us. Like I say, they were alright. Tinsley's alright.

Too many fucking Wednesday Pigs, but it's alright.

When I got to the shops, Gary and Hastey were waiting. We met there for every home game. All three of us were old hands. We'd started following the Blades in the First Division relegation season. A couple of seasons in the Second, then relegation. The season before we'd been runaway leaders of the Third until Christmas. On Boxing Day, the Pigs beat us 4-0 and we dropped to mid table in the end. Unbelievably, things got worse. In our career as football supporters we'd experienced lows that fans of some teams see only in their darkest nightmares. It had come down to the final judgment.

Last day of the season.

SHEFFIELD UNITED V WALSALL

Fifth bottom V Fourth bottom.

United win: they stay up.

United draw: they stay up.

Walsall win: United go to the Fourth for the first time in their history. Rock bottom. The madhouse. Sheff United are shit—official.

Hastey and Gary both had bottles of Merrydown. Hastey was hyper.

—Up forrit Ando?

—Yeah.

—This is it man. The turnin point. The good times are

9

comin back to t'Lane. We're stayin up, then Peters'll sort em out. Next season, we'll be up there. Get some o that down thy.

I took a long drink from the bottle while he carried on babbling. Hastey was a fanatic. The Blades were his religion. According to him, United were the biggest club around; they just needed the right man to lead them back from their spell in the wilderness. I was a Blade through and through and, like all football fans, I took the odd trip to Fantasy Island, but not like Hastey. He felt it more than any of us. He lived and breathed the Blades. Most of the lads admired that, but I felt sorry for him.

We divvied up our cash to get a few cans. I was skint bar my match money, but it was alright. Gary had weighed in some scrap and Hastey—his parents had a few bob. He never went short. Hastey got six cans of McEwans and another bottle of Merrydown. Gary was dead quiet; like he had something on his mind. Obviously he had the match on his mind, we all did, but there seemed to be more to it than that. Gary Burke was the straightest lad I knew. Salt of the Earth. Do anything for his mates. Never leave you to stand on your own. He was the only lad in Tinsley who didn't have a nickname, nobody even called him Gaz. Weird that. I knew that if something was bothering him, it had to be serious shit. I didn't say anything.

Hastey more than made up for Gary in the conversation. He was preaching the gospel to our wavering souls, reeling off statistics and precedents: 'Walsall hadn't won away since October. United hadn't been in the bottom four all season.' God he was pissing me off. Why couldn't he suffer in silence, like everybody else?

The beers went down and we got the bus up town. I was relieved. I wanted to get it over with.

The ride up town always made me wonder what it must be like for away fans who got off the motorway at Tinsley. All the way to the city centre, there was nothing but works and wasteland. And the smell. Most of them would never have seen anything like it. It was grim and hard, but it was ours—welcome to the Steel City, you faggots.

Dixie and Chip had gone up early to meet the crew in the Bell. They always used to come to the games with us, but Dixie was a social climber. Desperate to be one of United's top boys he was. By the time the bus got in, it was gone one. The three of us headed straight for London Road. Pre-match, The Lansdowne was the place to be for anyone with thug leanings. By the time we arrived, it was packed with a Who's Who of Sheff United bad lads.

The Lads. Our Boys. Whenever you saw a gap appear on the opposition's terrace or a scuffle in the seats, you knew it was them. To the youngsters, they were the heroes of the game. Since we'd been Blades, the team had achieved nothing. The great moments had been off the field (although they did occasionally spill on to it). The riot at home to Leicester, the battle with the police at Hull. They were our glory games.

Gary went to the bar while me and Hastey looked for Dixie and Chip. They were easy to find. A group of the main men were enthusiastically discussing the weekend before's encounter with Wednesday's boys, up West Street. Dixie and Chip were on the edge of the conversation; not saying anything but nodding and laughing on cue.

Dixie just winked when we turned up. You could tell he didn't want to be seen hanging about with a bunch of shitty sixteen year olds. He was a shitty sixteen year old himself, so it was important for him to make an impression in front of the lads. Dixie's only ambition was to be one of the boys. A top lad. One of the faces with a nickname that all the juniors look up to. Kids reach an age when they realise they're never going to play for United. Dixie was a dodgy cunt: into anything bent, always carried a blade. It wasn't enough for him. He wanted to be a star. When your crew pulls off better results than your team does most weeks, being a top lad has a lot of glamour attached to it. Of course, I didn't have to do that. I was going to play for the Blades.

We stayed in the Lansdowne for a couple of pints. Dixie and Chip spent the time hanging on every word their idols uttered. Chip was a sad bastard. A big dopey cunt with a speech defect, he followed Dixie round like a dog. Dixie put up with him because he was the hardest cunt in Tinsley. A useful accessory if you're a cocky little gobshite.

Some of the boys gave Gary some shit.

—Nah den bone'ead. Mugged any grannies today?

—If tha keeps sniffin that Evo, thy air'll never grow back.

They were only pissing about, but they were out of order. Gary ignored them. He was above all that. Dixie and Chip were laughing. That pair of cunts wouldn't even be able to spell the word loyalty.

The match was what you'd expect from the two worst teams in the Third Division; total shite. There was a decent crowd, about 16,000, but in a ground that holds 45,000 it doesn't seem that many. So quiet it was eerie. Everyone tense. I was never a singer anyway. Always saw that as the domain of scarfers and sad cases, and I didn't buy the stuff about it being worth a goal start. Once the whistle blew, it was up to the team: they were up to it or they weren't.

Ten minutes from time, the muted celebrations start. The game is drifting to its inevitable conclusion: a boring 0-0 draw. Half hearted chants of 'Stayin Up, Stayin Up'. A few people start drifting off. The vultures. The ones who've come so that they can say they were there the day the Blades went down. The rest are praying we'll hang on. Hoping to confirm that we really are third rate contenders, not fourth rate nonentities.

Four minutes left. The ball's played into United's box. A

Walsall player controls it. He runs at MacPhail. He falls. The ref points to the spot. Conroy dives, but the penalty beats him.

SHEFFIELD UNITED 0 WALSALL 1

Instantly, the mood changes. Anger and hostility. Some cunt is going to get it for this. Every touch by a Blades player draws roars of abuse disguised as encouragement. Hastey is close to meltdown. I glance at Gary and catch his eye. His look mirrors mine; silent resignation. Disappointment is all we've ever known. We shouldn't have expected anything else.

United are pushing towards the Shoreham Kop where we are standing. A ball's played into the packed penalty area. Appealing hands fly up.

Handball. Penalty.

Relief, that's the only word for it. As they say: the fans go wild. Me and Gary hug each other. Hastey jumps on top of us like a maniac. It's going to be alright. Tony Kenworthy, our regular penalty taker, is out injured. Don Givens places the ball. No sweat. Givens is a veteran. Plays at the top level. Irish international. This is small beer to him.

Givens strides up.

Givens shoots.

The most feeble spot kick in the history of world football

rolls into the hands of the Walsall keeper.

The final whistle sounded. The fans went really wild. The coppers were expecting something. Every year there was a pitch invasion at the last match and when we went down, which was getting pretty regular, it always turned violent. A police line was formed in front of the away fans at the Lane end. The Walsall team took a few kicks and punches on the way to the safety of the tunnel.

We stormed the pitch and got caught up in the mob. It wasn't just the crew, it was everybody. They'd be the ones who got nicked, the civilians. The ones who were big on principle but lacked experience of 'mindless violence'. Years of frustration and pain were bubbling over. Somebody had to pay. It was horrible. The worst had happened. There was nothing anyone could do to change it.

After a few minutes, I found myself sitting in the South Stand. Gary was next to me. Fuck knows where Hastey had gone. All around us were small groups of Blades. Some crying. Others, like us, stunned. We didn't even look at each other. There was nothing to say.

The mob on the pitch lacked focus. They were desperate for a scapegoat. Somebody to vent their fury on. A wedge of them charged the stand. It was the chairman and directors, they'd sold us out. No money for players. The police were out of position. The evil board theory spread like wildfire. Anyone with a suit on got a pasting. The coppers waded in with their truncheons drawn. Horses charged from the back.

It took the coppers about twenty minutes to clear the ground. It was the usual crowd violence deal. A lot of milling about. One bloke charges. Everyone charges. Brutality. Coppers charge. Everyone runs. Start again. I heard later that some of them had got far enough to kick the boardroom door in. You hear a lot of stuff like that though.

Me and Gary walked back to town in silence. I didn't want to go home. There was no way I'd be able to put up with our old man, I'd end up decking the bastard. I knew Dixie and Chip would be staying up town. As soon as Wednesday got back, the lads would be off up West Street after them. Dixie had to be there. He needed the brownie points.

—Are tha doin owt tonight Gary?

It was the first time either of us had spoken for nearly an hour.

—I'm supposed to be goin to a party at Wincobank wi Barbara. Why, what thy up to?

—Nowt. I dunno. I'm just not in t'mood for goin ome. I fancy getting fuckin wrecked.

—That's about t'best idea I've eard all day.

It took us half an hour to walk up to Attercliffe. We could get into most pubs but drinking in the street was still more natural to us. Anyway, Gary was down to the last fiver of his scrap money. That would have got us four pints each in a boozer. In the offie, it bought enough Badger bitter to sink a barge.

We set up camp on the wall next to the Washford chippy. A very popular spot for the discerning outdoor drinker. Views of the River Don to the rear and Attercliffe Road to the front. This meant that you could wave people you knew off the bus to Tinsley.

After a few cans of cheap beer, the world wasn't such a bad place. It was the first time me and Gary had talked all day. Earlier on, it had been too tense and Hastey had been rattling on ten to the dozen. We even laughed a bit. That's what separated us from the Wednesday Pigs: having a sense of humour. Well, that and having intelligence, style and a personality. And we didn't wear cagoules or take sandwiches and a flask to away games.

Getting badgered was just what the doctor ordered. Sometimes, you've just got to sit down with your mates, the ones you trust, and get slaughtered. Gary knew that too. If he'd gone off to that party with his bird, he would have snapped. It would've been full of Pigs giving it the big one and part-time Blades acting gutted. Barbara would've been no help either. Gary had been seeing her for about a year. She seemed a right enough lass, but word had it she was a bit of a tart. From somewhere round Kimmy Park I think, I wasn't sure because going out with your lass and hanging about with your mates were two things you didn't mix. You set aside different nights for each.

The night after relegation to the Fourth Division, because of a missed, last minute penalty, was definitely a lads' night.

The Badger and the bullshit started flowing. I started talking about my glittering future career in football. It was something I didn't go on about much. Most of my mates were looking at the dole or a YOP scheme. By signing apprentice forms with United I'd landed the dream job of everyone I knew. If I went on about it, it'd look like I was bragging. If I asked people what they were doing, it looked like I was rubbing their noses in it. Gary was different. He was a real mate. He was chuffed for me. I could talk to him. I wanted to know if he'd got anything, but I didn't want to put him on a downer. He read my mind.

—I've got a job … Treeton pit. I got a letter this morning. Barbara's dad sorted it for me.

—Sound. You'll be earnin more than me.

—Aye. I suppose.

I left it at that. If I'd carried on I would've come over all patronising. The pit was a good job. A job for life. Decent money too. Fact is, unless you're a complete arsehole or one of the lucky few like me, any job you get when you're sixteen is a letdown. I remember when we were in the infants, the teacher asked everybody what they wanted to do when they grew up. I'd wanted to be a footballer, Gary had been one of a group of astronauts. Good job, the pit is.

Hastey arrived in the nick of time. We were running

short on beer and light relief when he saw us, off the bus. Me and Gary were well gone. It was knocking on for ten o'clock.

We creased up when Hastey came, as we'd been speculating on what had happened to him. The smart money was on a heart attack or spontaneous combustion. As always he had money in his pocket, and insisted on taking us to the Dog and Partridge for a few. He must've emptied his mam's purse that week.

Every night's disco night in the Dog, but Hastey had a tale to tell. He'd bumped into Dixie after the match and stayed up town with the lads.

Over a soundtrack of Landscape, Shaky and those Stars on 45, he told us about his night of Pig hunting and rolling over cars. Most of it was bollocks, but it had us hooked. I didn't buy into the cult of the crew, but I always liked to hear about a good result for United. I knew that, really, Hastey had spent a few hours hanging about, being moved on by the coppers, but the match and the beer made me want to believe his war stories.

Getting out of it was the plan and we succeeded. I got home about half three. We got a lock-in at the Dog, then Hastey shouted a taxi back to Tinsley.

I spewed up a couple of times at the pub, and felt a lot better for it. When I got into bed, the room was hardly spinning at all.

The worst had happened. Childhood illusions were dead

in the water, but so fucking what? Can't turn back the clock. Got to get on with it. Like Gary said: relegation meant a clear out. Got to be a new manager too. If Martin Peters is ten years ahead of his time, the future must be a dark and depressing place. United had too many old farts, that's why we'd got into the shit in the first place. If I got my act together, a first team chance was there for the taking, then ... who knows?

Like I said. Nothing like getting pissed with your mates once in a while.

Wimbledon (a)

—I was drivin dahn Streatham Igh Road the ovva night when I sees this black tart, so I pulls over and she says, 'You can take me ome for twenty quid.' I says, 'Fack off. Why the fack would I want to go to Africa at this time of night?'

The crowd went wild. Big Billy Brockley, overweight, self-satisfied Cockney, was storming the gig. These were his people. The 1995 Wimbledon and Roehampton Sporting Club's charity dinner. Five course meal, brandy, cigars, three guest speakers and an auction. Thirty five quid a head; all proceeds to local youth sports clubs. As I was on the top table, I had to make a show of enjoyment, even though Big Billy's gags were so old it's a wonder English Heritage didn't prosecute him for unlawful excavation.

My father in law had got me the gig. He was one of the local bigwigs. Jackie leaned on me to do it. Ever since I'd packed up playing, I'd been looking for direction. The journalism was going OK, especially the radio, but I was a long way off the Alan Hansen bracket. Like she said: after dinner speaking was 'another avenue to be explored'. Course, she was right, but I wasn't keen on anything that involved her dad.

I'd been introduced as 'Former Millwall star and top radio personality Paul Andrews'. If only it was that simple.

—A geezer got ran over larst week. He wakes up in the ospital and the doctor says, 'Do you want the good news or the bad news?' The geezer says, 'What's the bad news?' Doctor says, 'You lost a lot of blad in the accident so we ad to give you a trarnsfusion. We didn't ave enaff white blad so we ad to give you sam coon blad and sam Paki blad.' The geezer says, 'That's facking terrible. What's the good news?' The doc says, 'Your dick's grown eight inches and you're top of the Southwark housing list.'

Roar of approval mixed with applause. He knew what the audience wanted. Middle aged Sarf London boys who'd made good 'froo ard work wiv no elp from nobody.' And moved to the suburbs: 'too many efnics up there now.' This was their big night of the year. Trade in the golf sweaters and the bar at the local for a roast chicken dinner in a draughty sports hall. A chance to tell the others how well they were doing and to make a few contacts. A chance to get shitfaced and mourn the passing of Winston and the Richardsons. The good old days on the old manor.

—It was tough, but you knew where you were with people.

—Not now, not since the schwartzers moved in.

—And the council. Lesbian karate. I ask you.

—Those MOTs. Ow many can you let me ave?

—I was in the back of the car, wiv sam tart larst night. She says, 'I want you to hurt me Billy.' So I slammed her tit in the door, threw her out and drove off wiv er andbag.

My turn hadn't gone down as well as Billy's. To be honest, I was glad about that. I'd done alright though. I didn't enjoy it, but there was money in this game. Not tonight as it was for charity, but I reckoned I could face it once in a while to pay the bills. It'd make Jackie happy anyway. She was really worried about me.

I'd been lucky to go second, after the president of some rugby union club who'd mistakenly thought that a sporting club dinner would want to hear about sport. His considered address on the implications of professionalism went down like the Belgrano.

I served up what the punters wanted from a washed up pro. Crap jokes about local teams and top name anecdotes. Throw in a few references to how grim it is up North and you're on a winner. The Harry Bassett stories got a good response. One of their own, wasn't he? And he was being touted for the Palace job. My Vinny Jones stuff got laughs too. I felt a bit guilty about that. Vinny's a top bloke and I've spent years telling people how under rated he is as a player, but I spent that night telling those cunts what a Neanderthal he was for a few cheap laughs. I suppose he'd understand.

I finished off with the George Best anecdote. I said he'd told it to me personally, but I'd never even been in the same room as the great man. It was the one everyone knows: George goes to the casino with Miss World, wins a fortune at roulette then goes to his room and calls room service. Some old guy comes in with the champagne and sees Miss World spread naked on the bed, surrounded by mounds of cash. He turns to George and says, 'I don't know, Mr Best. Where did it all go wrong?'

They'd all heard it before, but they still roared with laughter. Perfect story, pushes the right buttons. Pissheads are fun. Birds are gagging for it if you're successful. George Best, perfect geezer. You've either got talent or you haven't. Take away everything I own, put me back in Peckham and in a couple of years I'd have a new business and a ticket for the Wimbledon and Roehampton Sporting Club charity dinner.

—Two old Jews walking dahn the street when a BNP meeting turns aht. Isaac says to Morrie, 'Vey, we're going to get mugged here.' Morrie says, 'I think you're right. Here's that fifty quid I owe you.'

The strained smile was starting to hurt by now. I'd done my bit and wanted to get off. My mood wasn't helped by the amount of brandy I'd put away. Spirits always made me tetchy. I wondered how many of the 'sportsmen' in the hall had seen me play. Probably not that many. Most of them seemed like glorified versions of our old man. They must've been gutted that Millwall were top of the First. They could still enjoy Palace flogging their best players and bumping

24

along near the bottom I suppose.

—So the copper's chasin this shirtlifter dahn the street. He dacks dahn this back alley and the copper follows im. It's a dead end and there's no sign of the puff anywhere. This copper says, 'Right. Cam aht nah. Cos if I've got to look for yer, I'm gonna stick my truncheon right ap your facking ringpiece when I find yer.' And this little excited voice pipes up, 'I can't wait. Look in the dustbin.'

I joined in the rapturous applause that greeted the end of Billy Brockley's spot. For me it was a gesture of relief rather than approval, but my relief was short lived. It wasn't knocking off time yet. I'd forgotten about the charity auction, compered by Big Billy Brockley.

This was painful. How anyone could raise a smirk at the cracks about Wimbledon's crowds during the bidding for the executive box tickets is beyond me. The signed football I'd brought (cue BBB: 'Any Millwall fans in? Make yourselves at ome, smash a few chairs') went for eighty quid. Everything went for a good price. 'Well it's for charity innit. For the young uns.'

No item was too tatty to start a bidding war between a few drunken pillars of the community. They were all doshed up, they were all caring and big-hearted, they were all arrogant cunts pissed out of their minds on cheap brandy and keen to let the others know who was boss. At last it was over. The cricket bats, tickets, dartboards and golf lessons had all gone. The chairman announced the amount of money that had been raised. Home time.

Home was the last thing on the minds of the guests. For them dinner time was over but boozing time was only just beginning.

Small groups started to form around the hall as they moved from their allocated places. The stench of cigars, brandy and bullshit grew thicker. It was time to make my excuses and leave.

Jackie's dad was standing nearby, chatting with a few of the other top bods. I guessed he was pitching for a job. Have you ever met a builder who isn't? He ignored my excuse and insisted I had one for the road.

—You dun good tonight Paul. I've been to plenty of these dos, and I've seen a lot worse. Very good. Specially for a first attempt.

—Cheers Bob.

—What's that yer say? It was is first time. Well you've dan yourself proud san.

I thanked the well-wisher.

—Still playing for Millwall are you Paul?

Arsehole.

—No. I've retired.

—What you up to nah then?

Fuck off arsehole.

—This and that. Ya know.

—Yeah, I know.

The fat bastard gave me a wink and rejoined the group.

At least he didn't push it. I was doing nothing. Well next to nothing. The radio thing was promising, but who knows? Finishing as a player is worse than leaving school. All the same questions. 'Are tha workin sun?' If you're not you get pity. Patronising comments from real adults. Men who have proper jobs. If you show any ambition or want to do something out of the ordinary you get sneered at. I've lived out their dreams, so now they want to get even. You can see it in their eyes. 'Welcome to the real world, Mr Footballer. Run a pub. Go bankrupt. Kiss my arse.'

I felt somebody staring at me. When I turned round I saw a big feller. Looked to be about forty, built like a shithouse door. He walked over and offered me his hand. Seemed a bit nervous.

—I've seen you play many times. It's a pleasure to meet you.

The bloke had a firm handshake and the hint of a Yorkshire accent: both good signs. We talked for about ten minutes. To be more accurate, the big feller talked for about ten minutes. He was a Blade, from Woodhouse originally. I just stood there while he lovingly reeled off his recollections of my best performances. Didn't ask the 'what are you up to' questions either. I liked this guy a lot. My ego needed a boost.

Eventually, Jackie's dad turned round. He knew my number one fan.

—Alwight, Dave. Enjoyed yerself tonight?

—Yeah, smashing Bob. Best do I've bin to with the club.

—I ope you ain't been a naughty boy Paul. Cos eel ave yer.

I stared back. This was over my head. The big bloke looked embarrassed.

—E ain't told you oo e is, as e? Paul: this is Dave Knowles, better known to his friends as Detective Chief Inspector Dave Knowles.

I must have looked shocked because Jackie's dad started pissing himself laughing.

—Watch im Paul. Eel ave yer given arf the chance.

Bob turned back to his conversation. The copper was looking shame-faced.

—I'm sorry. I should've told you who I was.

—Don't be daft man. You did tell me who you are: a Blade from Woodhouse. Just cos you're a copper dunt mean you should ave it tattooed on yer ead.

He loosened up and we got back on to the serious issues. What was my best goal? Which was the best side I ever played in?

Nice bloke, Dave. We ended up chatting until kicking out time.

Must be weird being a copper. You can't tell people straight off what you are. I mean, that's the first thing most people ask you: 'What do you do?' Tell the truth and half the people hate you from the off and the other half are on their guard in case you're after something. Tough one.

28

Nobody forces them to join up though and, let's face it, most of them are bastards when it comes down to it.

Driving home was a nightmare. I was sure that there was a short cut to Tulse Hill but I didn't know where it was. The A205 was my only real option. I wanted my bed. The South Circular looks a fairly straightforward proposition on a map, but in the flesh, it's like a theme park based on hell.

I'd been driving more than I ever had, but still hated it. Couldn't understand how anyone could say they enjoyed it. The whole macho Jeremy Clarkson deal. When it came to getting from A to B, I was a confirmed public transport and taxi man. The road was full of impatient arseholes. Real surprise in London, that is. I had enough trouble with those filter junctions at the best of times.

Why did Jackie need a car this size in the first place? I made a mental note to lay off the brandy in future.

I slipped up at the lights at Streatham Hill. It wasn't my fault. I stayed in the right-hand lane all the way up to the crossroads. I didn't know it was for turning right only. When I got up to the junction the lights were changing to red. If I'd not gone the cunts in the other lane wouldn't have let me over. Never do in London. Even if they want to, they've got some bastard up their arse going berserk.

So I jumped the light. So what? No harm done. I was on Christchurch Road. Five minutes and I'd be home.

I hoped that Jackie was asleep. OK, the gig hadn't been a disaster but I didn't fancy talking about it. She'd be too enthusiastic and it would end up as another row. Better to leave it for a while.

I saw the flashing blue light in the mirror. This was all I needed. I pulled up. The only way out of this was some serious arse kissing. I needed my licence for work. It had been at the bottom of the drawer for years. Great timing. Fucking typical. I wound down the window and got my retaliation in first.

—I'm really sorry. I know why you've pulled me. I was in the wrong lane and couldn't get over, I thought it'd be safer to go.

—Is this your car sir?

Perfect. A fucking robot.

—It's the wife's, but I'm insured for it.

—Can I see your licence please sir?

I gave it to him. I was waiting for it. 'Been drinking have we? Blow into this ... I'm afraid I'll have to ask you to accompany me to the station.'

Brixton was the nearest nick. Sure to be full of interesting characters at that time of night.

—Paul Andrews.

—Yeah.

—I thought I recognised you. Bet you wish you were still playing. Top of the league and all that.

Stupid fucking remark.

I smiled and agreed. This could turn out alright. He was only a young lad. Bit overawed I'd say. His questions were

30

more nosey than investigative. I played along.

—Oh ya know. This and that. I've just finished an after dinner speaking engagement. Wimbledon and Roehampton Sporting Club. Dave Knowles was there. He's from your nick isn't he?

The name drop was maybe pushing it a bit, but the lad bought it. You could tell he aspired to that kind of shit. Rank, charity dinners, mingling with the great and good.

He let me off. I'd have to produce my documents ('Sorry Paul, already called it in, procedure') but no breathalyser. I was well over the limit and he knew it. Anybody else, any of those other fakers from the dinner; he would've nicked them without even thinking about it. They might have the dosh and the status but so what? They'd not get that kind of respect in a million years. When was the last time you saw a kid in a playground pretending to be a small businessman?

Jackie was out cold when I got home. Everything had turned out as well as could be expected, I suppose. I got into bed and thought about the future. Jackie rolled over but she didn't wake up. She wasn't showing yet. Soon I'd have to start telling her how beautiful pregnant women look. We'd be alright. Jackie meant well. I just wished she'd get off my case sometimes. I'd show the fucking lot of them.

I wasn't finished. Not by a long way.

24th February 1983

Bournemouth (a)

The taxi arrived at noon. Even with bad traffic, it only took twenty minutes to get from Tinsley to Bramall Lane. I'd allowed for and hour and a half, just to be on the safe side.

It was really happening. I'd always believed I was capable of making it and now it was happening. After a first year game at school, some bloke had come up to me and asked if I wanted a game with the Throstles, United's nursery team. Then it had all gone to plan: schoolboy forms at fourteen, Sheffield boys, apprentice terms when I left school.

In my first year I'd established myself in the youth team. Central midfield. I was a stocky lad and my game was based on aggression as much as skill. Having said that, I was a very good passer of the ball. In my schooldays I used to fancy myself as a new Billy Bremner or Archie Gemmill. Once it becomes your living, you don't really have heroes any more, but if I modelled my play on anyone at that time it was Souness. For my money, he was the complete midfielder.

To be honest, being a pro was a bit of a let-down. As a

kid you dream of the packed houses, the big matches. For an apprentice, the reality is sweeping up, cleaning boots and long minibus trips to empty grounds, with fish and chips on the way home. And everything gets so technical. It's not a game any more, it's a job. The coaches hammer the system they want to play into you. Tell you exactly what is expected of you and what is unacceptable. Just like any other firm.

Fans moan that there aren't any characters in the game these days. You don't see many maverick bus drivers or shop assistants with a free role either. Business is business. You do as the boss says or you're out.

Things really started to go well in my second year. I'd played for the reserves more than the youth team. You actually got a couple of hundred turning up to watch in the Central League and you were playing against some stars. Guys you'd heard of who were coming back from injury and stuff. More importantly, you got known by the first teamers and noticed by the Boss.

I could feel that my time was coming. The season before, Ian Porterfield had been brought in as manager and the Blades had walked the Fourth Division. There had been a real buzz around the club. Attendance records were being smashed and Hastey's sleeping giant theory looked to be about right.

This year was a different story. Instead of storming through the Third, we stalled. The first team couldn't put any kind of run together and, come the New Year, it was obvious that mid-table obscurity was all we could look forward to. The local papers were full of letters accusing the players of a lack of passion and fighting spirit.

I'd been training with the firsts since the beginning of February. On the Wednesday morning the Boss told me to see him in his office after the session. My mind started racing. I was down to play in the stiffs at home to Wolves on the Saturday. The first team were at Bournemouth. Ray McHale and Mike Trusson had both been carrying injuries. I could cover for either of them.

When I went to see him, Porterfield asked me if I thought I was ready. It was the most stupid fucking question I'd been asked in my life. Ever since I could remember I'd been preparing for it. I managed to stay calm while he gave me a speech about taking opportunities and responsibility.

Predictably, the taxi got me to the Lane an hour early. We were staying in Bournemouth for two nights. Travel down Friday afternoon, home on Sunday. This wasn't usual but, at the meeting the day before, the Boss had lectured us on the need to develop team spirit. A weekend on the piss in Bournemouth was to be the starting point.

I didn't want to be too early so I got the driver to drop me off at the Lansdowne, where I sat in the corner nursing a coke for half an hour. It was the first time I'd been in for about a year. I didn't think it would do my prospects with the club any good if word got round that I hung around with 'the mindless few who drag the name of Sheffield United through the mud'. I hardly saw any of my old mates.

You just can't go uptown on the piss with the lads. Too much hassle. Too much to lose. I tended to go out with other lads from the Youth team. They were in the same boat. We weren't angels but we knew the score; no room for mavericks in the game etc. I did phone up Gary the night before. He was made up. Said he would've come down but he had something on with Barbara. Typical.

By the time I entered the players' lounge there were a few of the lads around. A couple had been in for treatment and had teeshirts and trackies on. I hadn't been sure about what to wear for the trip. I'd gone for my sports jacket, button-down and a pair of chinos. Very smart but not overdressed, as though I'd not given it any thought. As it turned out, most of the lads were wearing jeans and training kit, but it didn't matter. I thought I looked the part.

I was dying to ask Trusson how his groin felt but he would've seen straight through me. I mean, it's not the kind of question you ask a bloke you hardly know.

One by one the team arrived. Some buoyant, some quiet; like any other bunch of blokes turning up for work. A few took the time to have a quick word with me. They all knew how I was feeling and most wanted to help me. There were some exceptions. After all, there are only eleven shirts to fill. A new kid on the block meant someone could be on his way out. You're promising, then you're nearing your peak, at your peak then ... who knows? It's the way of the world. Some lads have trouble dealing with it.

On the coach I read my book. I didn't want to piss people off by trying to be one of the boys straight off. That would come with time.

I was reading '1984' by George Orwell. I thought that loads of people would be talking about it over the coming year and I always liked to be on the ball. As expected, I got some stick for being a bookworm, but it was all good natured. I laughed it off. I never bought into the working class, proud to be thick thing. That kind of shit puts you on a one way ticket to the Club with our old man. It wasn't as though I was a sad case. I read the odd book, but I had a life as well.

'1984' is a top book; really makes you think. I didn't read it properly until months later. On the way to Bournemouth it was my cover so that I could earwig the other conversations. There was one main topic, the Summer Tour.

Rumour had it that United had been invited to play in Brunei as guests of the Sultan; the richest man in the world. Couple of matches, few days in the guest wing of the

37

palace, stopover in Thailand on the way home. It was only a whisper but it was getting louder by the minute. My eyes were looking at the story of Oceania but my thoughts were in Eastasia.

The timing seemed perfect. In the Summer my contract was up for renewal. As I'd fought my way up to being a fringe player a good new deal seemed a certainty. They'd have to take me on tour as a sweetener.

This was it. Playing for the Blades, world travel, good money. What more could a Tinsley lad wish for? It didn't take long to get round to that. A couple of the lads had been to the Far East before. Their abiding memory—Sex, and plenty of it. Things were coming together at just the right time.

I don't want to go off on a 'when I were a lad it were grim up North' kick, but I'd never stayed in a hotel before that weekend.

Nice joint it was too, the Morrison. Over on the West Cliffs. I knew I could get used to that lifestyle. My room-mate was Dougie Baker, a left back known as Ginger for the obvious reasons. He'd been with the club for a couple of years. They'd picked him up on a free from Rangers. I assumed that I was rooming with him because he was only a couple of years older than me and we'd played in the stiffs together. Ginger never stopped talking. He spoke in detail on a huge range of subjects from Glasgow's a really hard city to Glasgow's a brilliant place and including anything else about Glasgow in between.

It was a relief to go down for the meal.

A few of the lads asked me if I'd ever been to Glasgow and laughed. I'd been stitched up. Fair enough. Last in and all that.

I'm sure I must have slept at some time that night, but I don't know when.

All I can remember is staring at the ceiling, thinking about the game. That Ginger cunt snoring all night didn't help. I hoped that me and him sharing wasn't a permanent arrangement.

On the Saturday morning we all went out for a walk on the front. It's odd when you think about it. A group of well paid professional fellers being herded around, like window-licker kids on a trip to the seaside. When the Boss decided we'd had enough excitement it was back to the hotel for snap.

Over the scrambled egg he told us the team. Trusson had come through a fitness test, so he was starting. I had to make do with a place on the bench.

On the coach to the ground, Ginger played the old pro and tried to console me by telling me about how he'd been sub on his debut. I didn't pay any attention to the story but I'm sure it was set in Glasgow and lame as fuck.

Running out at Dean Court isn't what most kids dream

of but, on a warm, sunny afternoon, it'll do. During the warm up I tried to pick out someone I knew in the away end, but I couldn't. Dixie would be around somewhere. The South coast was stopover material for the crew. An ideal chance to cause mayhem and do some serious robbing.

AFC BOURNEMOUTH 0 SHEFFIELD UNITED 0

I was quite happy. I'd made my league debut. Colin Morris had felt a twinge in his knee when he pulled up sharp. The Boss didn't want to take any chances, after all, we weren't really playing for anything. In the 70th minute, Paul William Andrews, aged 18 years 111 days, came on as substitute to make his first appearance for Sheffield United Football Club.

Went like a flash that twenty minutes. I didn't really have much to do. Both teams were happy enough with a point. The important thing was, I didn't fuck anything up.

The highlight was the final whistle. Going over to the few hundred Blades behind the goal to milk the applause. I was one of them and they were saluting me. They'd come all this way to support me. Really I knew that, sad cases apart, they were a mob of lads who had used the match as an excuse for a mad weekend away, but it felt like they were there for me.

Most players have never been proper fans. They do

believe that the lads go away every week because they love the way the team plays. I allowed myself to be deluded for a day.

We got back to the Morrison at about half six. Porterfield had been quite happy with the performance. He had a few gripes but managers always have. He took me to one side and said I'd done well. A few of the lads did. It may have been my imagination but they seemed to be treating me differently. Like I was one of them. A few more under my belt and I would be. My mind wandered off to the seedy bars of Bangkok.

All the lads met in the bar at eight. Everyone was suited up. The Boss had told us we could do what we wanted. He came down and gave us a quick lecture about how we were representing the club as much when we were off the field as when we were on it, then left us to it. The squad split into two groups: those who were going into town and those who were staying in the hotel bar. The divide was pretty much single/married.

I opted to stay. I didn't want to get a reputation as a pisshead. Also there was a chance I'd bump into Dixie and the crew if I went out and that could lead to a list of disasters. Best to be cautious. Staying in, on top of reading a book, meant I took some stick, but I reckoned it was better to risk getting called a stiff for the time being. Once

41

the contract was sorted and we were on tour they'd be introduced to the real Paul Andrews.

At first it was a fairly standard night in the bar. Typical bloke stuff. Few pints while you go over the day's events.

—So I says to the little cunt. You try and go past me again an I'll break yer fuckin legs for ya.

I hardly said a word. For me it was a buzz just being there. I'd cracked it. Truly won the lottery of life: I was a United player.

The buzz started to wear off. To be honest I was a bit bored. This was the married crew, so they soon got on to the standard conversations: house prices, money, kids. Hardly the kind of stuff to set an eighteen year old's pulse racing. I started to look round the bar. It was full of what I would later come to recognise as your average Saturday night hotel crowd: old posh people and middle class couples dolled up for a 'special' meal out.

One table stood out from the rest. Two birds on their own. Looked to be in their early twenties. One was tall with short bleached blonde hair, stretch jeans, tartan blouse and a suede waistcoat. She was well tasty and her mate was even better. Short lass with really tidy black hair, done in a bob. She had a matching navy jacket and short skirt on. Lovely figure. Bit chunky but in all the right places.

It didn't take long for me to get sussed out. Ray had noticed me looking over.

—I think young Paul's in love.

42

Just looking.

—Get yirsen o'er there.

That set them all off. Married blokes are all the same. Casual sex is their favourite spectator sport. They're done with that caper but like to give the impression that, if they were single, they'd be up there like a rat up a drainpipe. Course, they don't have to bother. Steak at home, on tap and all that. At that age you don't see through that bullshit so easily. I think half of them believed it themselves.

—What's up with ya? If I didn't have a ring on my finger I'd be straight over there.

—But there's two of em.

—That shouldn't be a problem at your age.

Everyone laughed. Even Ginger Baker. He was only twenty but he had a wife, a kid and a mortgage already. The fact that his missus was a fat, sour faced old slapper didn't affect his membership of the smug married man's association.

I realised there was no way I was talking my way out of this one. Fuck it. I'd had a few pints. I drained my glass, then theatrically brushed down my crew-cut and adjusted my tie. My 'mates' all smiled expectantly. They reminded me of the way my granny looked when she watched It'll Be All Right On The Night.

I stopped at the target table. The girls were chatting and didn't notice me at first. At that moment I realised I had nothing to say. Lasses I'd been with before, you just sort of

43

ended up with them. You got talking to them, then, later on, you finished up snogging them. I had no experience in the lounge lizard, chat up merchant stakes.

They looked up and stopped talking.

—Alright. I wondered if you fancied a drink?

For about a month they stared at me like I was from another planet. Then the nice one smiled.

—Why not? Two vodka and tonics, large ones.

I walked to the bar and ordered the drinks plus another pint for myself. On the way back to the table I noticed the lads looking at me. I'd already got further than they expected and it felt good.

—There you go.

—Cheers. I'm Tina and this is Diane.

Diane, the tall bird, didn't seem too bothered about being friendly.

—My name's Paul.

—And what brings you to this fine establishment on a Saturday night Paul?

—I'm a professional footballer. I play for Sheff United. We played Bournemouth this afternoon.

You've got no idea how good it felt saying that. From Tina's reaction I could tell she was impressed. I'd suddenly changed from half-pissed Northern chancer to interesting professional athlete.

She was hooked. Wanted to know all about me. About my career. I didn't even have to make much up. Tina kept firing questions and hanging on my every word. This was more than I could have hoped for.

I didn't have to look round at the lads. I could feel their expressions. A shock result looked on the cards.

Tina was different class. She had a posh accent but she wasn't snotty. Diane looked bored and said nothing. I hoped she wasn't going to get in the way. I decided it was time to change the subject: talk about them, always a sound tactic.

—What are you down ere for?

—We're on a story. I'm a journalist, Diane's a photographer.

Diane smiled weakly. Turned out they worked for the News of the Screws. Tina's fascination with me started to make sense. She was fishing for titbits. I felt a mug. Having said that, she did seem to like me.

Tina insisted on shouting the drinks (expenses). Whatever happened, I was in a position to claim victory after that. Sexy bird gets beer in all night: a result in anybody's language. The lads would have to buy that.

Tina and Diane were on a gay vicar story. Some old boy over in Poole. Apparently he'd been having rent boys round his rectory. Tina said it was hypocritical. It was important to expose him.

—Yeah, disgusting.

She laughed.

—Not really. It's just a bit of scandal. The punters love a

dollop of sleaze with their cornflakes.

—Yeah, I suppose so.

—Dirty old bugger should've been a bit more careful.

By this time, I was feeling quite pissed. I had no idea how I was getting on with Tina. I wasn't used to this quality of opposition. She'd not been on the paper long. She'd been at the LSE (whatever that was) then worked on some local rag. The gay vicar was her best story so far, that's why she was so determined to nail him. She was a hard bitch alright. Great tits though.

I went to the bog. Keith was in there.

—How you gettin on?

—I reckon I'm gonna be the only Blade to score this weekend.

I regretted saying it straight away. Too smug, too arrogant and it made it look like I was definitely in. If I blew it I'd look a prize dickhead. Keith laughed, so I supposed it was alright.

When I got back, Tina was alone.

—Where's Diane?

—She's gone off to some club in town.

—Why dint you go wi er?

—Didn't fancy it. Anyway, I've got to be up early tomorrow. Got to go to church.

I clicked on and smiled.

—I'm going to have a drink up in my room. Would you like to join me Paul?

✫

The trip back to Sheffield was fantastic. I got loads of stick from the lads. I'd already been given a nickname: Warren, as in Beatty. They were all acting like little kids. Kept asking for a blow by blow account. I'm surprised they didn't ask to smell my fingers.

Tina had been great. I'd never met anyone like her. All the lasses at home were full of shit; all they thought about was what people thought of them, whether they were slaggy or tight. Tina was something else. So confident. She knew what she wanted and got on with it.

I wasn't stupid. I knew that I wasn't the best looking bloke in the world and a bird like Tina wouldn't look twice if I wasn't a footballer. Big deal. In a lot of ways, that made it better. She wanted me for what I'd made of myself, not because of some accident of nature. It's like all them rich old blokes with young birds. Do you really think they give a fuck what people say?

Me and Tina didn't bother exchanging numbers or anything. We fucked each other then both said cheers. Simple as that. We were young professionals on the way up. There'd be plenty more of this along the way for the pair of us. I hid behind my book; basking in jealousy and acclaim. Welcome to the big time.

QPR (a) 1st leg

The days of football clubs being a focal point of the local community are long gone. Manchester City could once attract crowds of 70,000 plus on a regular basis. Predominantly working men, from a small catchment area, these fans would walk or take the tram to the stadium. After a week of drudgery, Saturday afternoon was the time to be entertained.

The entertainment consisted of standing packed like sardines on a crumbling terrace with the bloke in front's leg for toilet facilities. The game meant everything because the lads in blue were ordinary fellers, like them. Underpaid workers who turned out, rain or shine, to do their best for City.

A look at their near neighbours at Old Trafford sums up the nature of contemporary football. Most United fans couldn't find Manchester on a map, let alone have a sense of community spirit.

Each home game, they travel to their Mecca, to see the idols that they watched on television as they grew up. The crowds have more in common with the audience at a recording of Gladiators, than the Maine Road hordes of yesteryear. The 'ordinary' fan is being priced out of the luxurious new grounds and replaced by affluent families, decked out in the official merchandise of the Red/Black/Blue and White/Grey Devils. The supermodel wages and lifestyles of Giggs, Cantona and co are light years away from your average Manc's lot.

It's time to face facts. Football is no longer a game; it's a business. Manchester United are a public company and it is their duty, as such, to produce a profit for their shareholders. Success on the park is part and parcel of this, so the interests of the 'club' and the fans converge in this area. However, we should always be aware that profit is the bottom line.

Against this background, Wimbledon's proposed move to Dublin makes perfect sense. The rules of free market economics tell us that, to survive and prosper, a firm must maximise its profits by exploiting its market. The most successful firms will be those that tap into new markets and offer a product which meets the needs of the consumers therein. American sports realised this years ago.

The Dublin Dons are a marketing man's dream. The Irish capital is the ultimate gap in the lucrative domestic football market. It is a potential colony crying out for an imperialist power to invade it. Since the beginning of the Jack Charlton era ...

—AAAARRGH!

—Shit ... It's alright, I'm coming.

I pressed 'command S' on the keyboard, then went into the front room, to see what the emergency was. Annie was sitting on the floor, next to the telly, bawling her head off.

—I know how ya feel luv. It's alright now. Daddy's ere.

I went over and picked her up. She didn't need changing, which was a huge relief. Jackie always looked like she genuinely enjoyed doing that. Parenthood really fucks up some people's grasp on reality. Annie had a little red mark on her head. It looked like she'd bumped into the telly. She was eighteen months and had just about got to grips with the walking thing. Pity she didn't seem any closer to developing a sense of direction. If Annie could bump into something, she would. I rocked her in my arms to stop her crying.

—Who's a little Klinsmann, eh? Telly ardly touched ya. Just want Daddy's attention, don't ya? You'll grow up wi a big nose and a centre parting. Yes you will.

Annie calmed down a bit. The bump on her head did look quite bad. Perhaps the telly had deserved a yellow card after all.

—Come on Annie. It's alright now. If ya keep gettin bumps like that, Daddy'll end up in prison with all the Cleveland people. We don't want that. No we don't.

Annie stopped crying. It must be my back street genes— the threat of the nick always smartened her up. After a few minutes, she started smiling. That made me feel better.

Having kids had never been on the agenda for me. Annie was an accident. Once she came though, I could see what all the fuss was about. That look they give you. Unconditional love. Then again, you do feed them, clothe them and put a roof over their head. Bit like having a dog really. I don't mean that.

I hoped that she'd get off to sleep, so that I could finish the article. It'd taken me ages to get started, but then it began to flow quite well. If all went to plan, I'd flog it to 'Goal' or 'Total Football'. Maybe 'When Saturday Comes', if I made it a bit more poncey.

I'd always fancied myself as a journalist. When I was at school, I'd been good at writing. English was the only O-level I got. Then again, I didn't exactly break my back trying in lessons. I knew what I was going to do when I left.

When I was playing, I was a bit of a teacher's pet to the hacks. I was always happy to give interviews. I wanted to learn all about it. They were pleased to accommodate me because ... er ... at the end of the day ... like ... they were ... obviously ... er ... ya know ... over the moon ... to interview a pro who ... ya know ... could string a sentence together.

Since packing up, I'd been trying to make a living at it. TV is a closed shop. If you haven't got 50 caps, they don't want to know you. Radio is a different story. While I was at Millwall, I'd built up a good relationship with the lads at South London Sound. I was getting bits of work off them;

all strictly casual though. If it all kept going OK, I was sure I'd get a contract eventually.

Writing's a tough nut to crack. I'd had a couple of pieces published, but all the bods in the business are dead elitist. Think you can't write unless you've spent three years at university. Can't accept that a working class, Sheffield lad can do it as well as them. Some of them know about the game, but they don't understand it. I was a pro. Spent all my working life involved in football. There's no way you can really understand the game unless you've been part of it; on the inside.

I knew that I could crack it, given time. I had no doubts about my own ability, but I felt Jackie was wavering a little. She always supported me, but I'd started to get the feeling she didn't take me seriously. Every day when she got in from work, she'd ask me what I'd been up to. Her tone of voice was like an infant teacher asking to see my picture. And as for when her mates came round ... I'd teach them snobby cunts to look down their noses at me. Like, what had they ever done?

I got the feeling that time was running out. In a few months, Jackie would be finishing work. Another accident. Even though she meant well, it always led to arguments when we spent time together. Any time she showed an interest in my 'career', I felt like she was putting me down.

—We're gonna show the fuckin lot on em. Aren't we Annie?

53

Annie was asleep.

I was glad when Jackie got home and I was off duty. The article had been doing my head in. I'd get it done by the end of the week; then it was off up to Sunderland on the Friday. Top of the table clash: Sunderland v Millwall. South London Sound were putting me up at a hotel for the night. If the lads could keep it up, it could turn into a regular thing. Promotion for Millwall would mean a contract for me.

Jackie got in at about seven. I was out of the door at ten past.

The ankle had been feeling miles better so I'd started running again. Nothing drastic; just a few miles, a couple of times a week. Jackie had been complaining, but she didn't understand. She thought I wanted to make a comeback. Said I was kidding myself, I'd only make it worse.

She didn't get it. I'd been a professional athlete. Sure I liked a pint and a ruby as much as anyone, but I hated being out of shape. Jackie had a point in a way; compared to most (just turned) thirty one year olds, I was a picture of health—but that wasn't enough. I was determined to keep my edge. The number of ex-pros who I'd seen turn into gutbuckets as soon as they packed up sickened me.

How could they let themselves go like that? The minute they've not got someone telling them what to do and wiping their arses for them, they go to pot. Pathetic. Check out all those 'Where Are They Now?' features. Sad it is. I wasn't going to end up as a failed small businessman.

I'm not saying I never thought about playing again. It'd be odd if I hadn't. You never lose those dreams. I bet even John Major sometimes drifts off and imagines he's one on one with Schmeichael, to win the Cup for Chelsea. I knew a comeback wasn't on the cards, so I didn't dwell on it. I had more important things to worry about. My address has always been: Paul Andrews, The Real World. You've got to get on with it.

The ankle felt OK as I pounded up Croxted Road. It was pretty mild for the time of year, but the darkness made Tulse Hill seem a depressing place to be. Jackie always told people that we lived in West Dulwich, but it was Tulse Hill really. I didn't buy into all that fashionable area shit. If urban deprivation was in vogue with her buddies, then she'd say we lived in Tulse Hill again. At a stretch, she might even get away with Brixton.

The streets were empty. I was glad of the peace. Jackie was my wife and I loved her; no question about that. But why couldn't she get it into her head that nobody cares about what goes on in other people's jobs? Office politics: load of bollocks. Anyone with a real job hasn't got time for all that petty, self important bullshit. You never hear about cleaners' politics or bus drivers' politics. Earn your money and then get away. Life's too short. As soon as she got through the door, Jackie had started on about her boss (Josh, need I say more?) That was my cue to put on my trainers, pull up my hood and hit the road.

I came out on Norwood Road and headed down to the junction. For a second, I thought about doing Herne Hill, then decided my old bones might not enjoy bouncing off the paving stones on the way down. The last thing I needed was a month with my foot in a bucket again. I took the easy option of a left down Dulwich Road, skirting the bottom of Brockwell Park. I ran down past the lido, then hopped over the wall into the park.

Brockwell Park: rolling greenery, playground, lido, bowling greens, tennis courts, open air theatre. In the summer, it's the natural daytime habitat of the average South London Sainsbury's user. On cold, dark nights, it takes on a different character; out of bounds to respectable folk. For them it becomes a nightmare landscape, ready to punish any unwitting, naive souls who risk a short cut. A bit like the dirty rag who used to prey on kids near water, in the old public information adverts (the show offs; they're the easiest, ha, ha).

Jackie told me I shouldn't run in the park at night. Too many muggers and 'God knows what else'. That's her middle class side—scared to death of the outside world. It's all in their heads. Most of these 'masters of the universe' types, who come slumming it to make the most of house prices, end up like it; locked away all night because they think every black kid they bump into is a mugger or a schizo with a blade. None of them admit it to each other, but us ex-street kids are like dogs. We can smell the fear on them.

It started spotting with rain. I was already breathing quite heavily. Maybe I was further from peak fitness than I'd admit to myself.

One lap of the park and I'd call it a day. Going straight home didn't really appeal, so I'd taken the precaution of bunging a tenner in my trackie bottoms. An hour in the Half Moon looked a good bet.

On the brow of the hill, I could see the outline of a big feller walking a dog. I think it was a dog anyway. It was such a shitty little thing, it could have been a hairy rat. No matter what time it is or what the weather's like, you always see some bloke out walking the dog. Same as if you walk home in the early hours, you see blokes sitting outside their houses in parked cars, having a fag. Any excuse to get away from the missus. It's easy to take the piss; but I was doing the same thing really. I suppose I'd have had to buy a pooch if my ankle hadn't healed up.

No sign of the legendary muggers. I'm sure they only exist in Jackie's pals' paranoia. When you're on holiday in other people's misery, everything outside the front door terrifies you. If you look at the figures, you realise how barmy it is. Growing up in a place like Tinsley teaches you what the real score is. Even if I did bump into a kid who fancied himself, I was confident I could deal with it. It'd be the worst night's fucking work the chancer ever did.

I felt my fists clenching. It was getting to me; all Jackie's bullshit. I was half hoping that some cunt would jump out and have a go. Fuck all chance of that though. No-one here but us wife-avoiding fitness fanatics.

The hill up from the playground was no fun. I could feel a stitch coming on. My body felt like it was going through one of Harry Basset's pre-season sessions. I cut right, on to the path. The rain was getting worse, and turning my ankle on the wet grass didn't bear thinking about.

About a hundred yards ahead, I could see a figure hanging about by the bushes, near the bowling green. He was up to no good. That wasn't paranoia, it was fact. The cunt was hanging about in a park, in the drizzle. You could tell from the way he just stood there that he was after something.

As I got closer, I could start to make him out. White kid, about twenty. Short cropped hair, baggy top, (no jacket) army trousers and white trainers. There was nothing to him. If he came it, I'd give it to him. No problem.

The cocky little twat was just standing there, staring straight at me. It crossed my mind that he was either carrying a blade or had a couple of mates hiding in the trees. He couldn't think he could roll me on his own, without the element of surprise. Fuck you, you little twat. I'd take the fucking lot of them.

I was right on him by now. Only about fifteen yards away. There was no way I was going to be intimidated by some little shit.

He probably thought I was some middle class arsehole. Somebody who'd shit themselves at the sight of a Stanley. Bad call, dickhead.

I slowed right down. Come on shithead. Let's have it.

The kid stared straight back at me, raising his eyebrows and licking his lips. I clicked on and carried on jogging past.

The lad wasn't after money. In Jackie's categories, he came under 'God knows what else'. He was looking for love. I glanced over my shoulder, to make sure he wasn't taking the piss out of me. The kid nodded towards the bushes. No doubt about it. He was on the level.

It may sound odd, but I felt good about it.

That kid wanted me so bad, he was willing to risk coming on to me. I could've been anyone. Anything could've happened.

I ran on into the dark. I turned left at the theatre and arrived back at the wall near the Herne Hill junction. I'd run off the stitch and I was ready for more. As I ran down beside the wall, I had an image of the kid in my mind.

It was so clear, it was untrue. Him standing there, piss wet through, raising his eyebrows at me. It'd never happened to me before. Sure I knew it went on, cottaging and all that, but I'd never been approached. I found myself

59

looking up to the brow of the hill, to see if he was still there. It was too far away for me to make anything out.

I'll admit that I was excited. Not sexually. No way had I ever got up to anything with another bloke. It was more a buzz. Like you get when you first drink in a boozer or go to an X-film underage. The buzz of being round something dodgy. I was running faster.

My head was full of sleaze. Strangers meeting up, nodding at each other, fucking, then off home. No bullshit. No pretending like with birds. Meet, fuck, home. No strings.

I started up the path, near the playground. My first lap had been nearly ten minutes earlier. I was almost sprinting and I didn't know why. I was desperate to see the kid again. I had no intention of doing anything with him. Not my scene. I didn't even want to talk to him, I just wanted him to be there. It's something I can't explain.

I couldn't see him. For some reason, I felt dejected. He must have got off. Can't blame him with the rain and all. Not many of his lot going to be out when it's raining. Or maybe he'd got lucky. Who cares? Fuck all to do with me.

Suddenly, he was there. The kid emerged from the bushes about fifty yards away. I was elated, then confused. I didn't know what was going on. The kid rubbed his cock and then walked back to the clump of trees and bushes. I carried on running. When I got to where he'd been, I looked over to the right. He was next to the bushes. He nodded at me, then disappeared into them.

I ran a few more steps, then slowed to a halt. I looked around. There was no one. Course there was no one around. It was December and it was raining. Who the fuck goes to the park at night, in the middle of winter?

Fuck it. Nobody's ever going to find out. I looked around again anyway. The coast was as clear as it would ever be. I slowly went over to the bushes. Another quick check around, then I went into the same gap as the kid had.

There was a clearing in the middle. The trees' shelter made it seem like coming inside. The kid was standing straight in front of me. What was I doing? I felt the grip of fear and excitement in equal measures. I was anxious for him to do something. This was his game. It was up to him to show me the rules.

—Hi.

—Hi.

—What's your name?

No way could I give him that.

—Tommy.

—I'm Lee.

Lee edged closer. Drops of water were falling from his head. He seemed to be looking for something in my eyes. I couldn't give it to him. I was petrified. Any urge I had to run away was being overruled by something stronger. Lee made his move.

—Are you up for it Tommy?

That question. It meant nothing but it meant everything. I didn't know exactly what was going to happen, but I knew I wanted it. I had to play the thing out. I couldn't bring myself to speak. I just nodded slightly. Lee was edgy. Goes with the territory. By now he was dead in front of me. Touching distance. He stretched out his right arm. His hand went up my training top and he touched my flesh. My heart was pumping.

Lee moved closer. He caressed my side. His hand moved to the waistband of my trackies. He slid it in. Lee firmly grabbed hold of my cock. Up till then, I hadn't realised that I had an erection, but it was rock solid against his hand. So hard it hurt. Lee flashed a smile. He could tell for certain that I was 'up for it'. He started to wank me; hard and fast. Properly, not like a lass. His confidence was growing.

—Do you like kissing Tommy?

I couldn't speak. He brought his head forward to kiss me on the lips, but I instinctively moved so he missed. No way could I do that. Lee sort of muzzled my cheek and neck. He whispered gruffly in my ear.

—I'm going to suck your cock, Tommy.

Lee got down on his knees and wrenched down my trackies. My dick sprang out. Lee took it firmly in his right hand. He leaned forward and teasingly licked around my bell-end with the tip of his tongue. He glanced up, rolled his eyes, then went down on it. A rush surged through my body. My head rocked back and my eyes closed. His tongue

62

and lips on my cock. His hands clenching my arse. Nothing else existed. It was unreal.

I came round and looked down. Lee's shaven head was vigorously jerking up and down on my dick. It was like watching a film. I reached down and stroked his scalp. It had that lovely suede feel.

I can't say for certain why it happened then. When you're charged up, it only takes the slightest thing. A cool breeze, rustling leaves, imagined voices. Who knows? It just hit me. All at once.

What the fuck is going on? I'm not a faggot.

Where's this going? No wife. No kids. No friends. Court case. No job. An outcast.

Lee let out a noise. Sounded like somebody who'd just tried a nice glass of wine. I'm putting my life on the line so this weedy puff can get some cheap thrills. He didn't give a fuck. Nobody. This wasn't worth it. Had to get away. Stop this. I tried to push his head away. There was no hair to grab on to. I got hold of his ears and jerked him back.

—No.

He looked confused. Kind of scared. Then he smiled.

—Like it rough do you Tommy?

Smart little bastard. My life was turning to shit and it's all just a fucking laugh.

—What's wrong?

I grabbed the cunt's ears and kneed him hard in the face. Pushed him back, then swung a few punches at him. The first couple connected, then he slumped backwards. I dived on top of him. Strangling and butting him at the same time. Five or ten. I don't know. I couldn't stop. Every time the head went in there was a thudding squelch. His face was all over. Blood gushing. Think I'm funny do you shithead? Not smiling now. I got up and stood over him. Sad wee cunt. He was writhing around then he started to push down on the ground like he was trying to get up. He might have started shouting and fuck knows what else. He was loose. I had to put him away.

I ran over and volleyed his head. He crumpled. I carried on booting his skull in. Maybe twenty times. Had to put him to sleep. Thank fuck I remembered only to use my right. Discipline. Never leaves you. Drilled in. Two footedness. Look after yourself.

It went quiet. I took a step back. Weird it was. There was just me. Me and this dead body. I knew he was dead straight away. I can't describe the feeling. Power? Immortality? It's like moving into a different class.

Eventually, reality kicked in again. Full gravity adrenaline hit. I wanted to do fifty things at once. Run for your life. Keep calm. Cover your tracks. I started grabbing handfuls of dead leaves and throwing them on the corpse. Longer it's undiscovered, the better. Fake mugging. I brushed off the leaves and rifled his pockets. No wallet. Cunt had a purse. Full monty this one. I pocketed it.

The coppers wouldn't buy it. Too brutal. Way over the

top for a mugging. Fuck it. It'd slow them down. No ID.

I covered the body again, then checked myself. OK. I unzipped my top and wiped my face on my teeshirt. Some blood. I managed to get rid of most of it. I straightened my clothes and put my hood up. The faggot had pulled it down when he'd been messing with me. I walked to the edge of the bushes and stuck my head out. Not a soul in the park. I slipped out on to the path.

In the ten minutes it took to run home, I lived more than most people do in a hundred years. I was flying. Had to watch how fast I was running. Had to blend in. No aches, no pain; pure exhilaration. Take your pick of drugs and you're still not close. Unbelievable. Once I hit the road, every passing car was a potential executioner. A future star witness for the prosecution. All wrapped up in their own stuff. Not a second glance for the jogger. Pits of despair to heights of ecstasy. Sixty, maybe, seventy times. I was more alive than anyone ever has been.

Home free. No problem. Through the door. I could hear Jackie. Upstairs putting Annie to bed. I dipped in the front room to check myself in the mirror. Not bad. Just a few dried blood spatters, on my face. I went through to the kitchen and rinsed my face, in case I passed her on the stairs, then stripped. I threw everything I'd been wearing into a carrier bag, then ran upstairs to the bathroom. I didn't say anything to Jackie. Nothing suspicious about that. Five minutes in the shower. Ten minutes staring at myself in the mirror. Staring into my killer eyes.

I knew I had to get out of the house. No way could I make neutral small talk with Jackie in that state. I was trembling. Not panic or fear. Pure mainline excitement. The telly went on downstairs. Jackie was out of the way. I went to the bedroom and threw on some old clothes. A button-down and a pair of slacks. Might need to duck in somewhere posh. I walked downstairs, clutching the carrier bag. I grabbed the car keys off the hall table and stuck my head round the front room door. She was spread out on the settee. Set for the night. Red wine, cream crackers; the full bit.

—How was your run?

—Alright. Look; I've got to nip out.

—Are you going to be late?

—I dunno. See ya later.

Like she gave a shit if I was late or not. If I'd told her everything about the park, she would've just nodded 'Mmm; that's nice'. Treated me like a daft kid.

The lights looked good. Lovely yellow colour. I needed to find a place where I could be anonymous. I followed the road due south. All I could see was his face. Stone dead. When I left, I'd had vague ideas about getting rid of the clothes. That soon went out of the window. Act in haste, repent at Her Majesty's Pleasure.

The search for clear roads led me to the M23. I didn't want to go too far. I came off at Gatwick. I'm not an idiot.

66

I had no intention of doing a Ronnie Biggs; never crossed my mind. All I needed was somewhere to hang out and get myself together.

I pulled in at one of the airport hotels and hit the bar. They're the same the world over. Plastic havens for tired business bods, caught in their own things. Minor movers and slight shakers. Nobody paid me any attention. Nondescript bloke in the corner, knocking back a few pints. Odd though: I had this strong feeling that they were all jealous of me, all wished they were me. I didn't say a word to anyone.

The incident kept replaying, over and over again, in my head. I didn't analyse it or fight it. I just watched.

The traffic was light on the way home. Not much reason for going into London at midnight on a Wednesday. I didn't mind driving when it was like that. The Mondeo can really trap, when you've got a bit of open road to aim at. Even Jackie's tapes sounded good. You've got to be in the mood to appreciate that kind of stuff.

2nd February 1985

Everton (h) FA Cup 4th Round

Running out on to the pitch that day was fantastic. Capacity crowd. Match of the Day cameras. Best team in the land as opposition.

Since we'd been drawn against Everton, Barnsley had been buzzing. The whole town had talked of nothing else. Old grannies; the lot. When we finally left the tunnel, the noise was deafening. Hope and release. Forget the strike for a day. You could get more than thirty thousand in Oakwell then. The big matches. They're what it's all about. Dreams can come true; if you can handle it.

I'd never been involved in a match with such a high level of interest. Two years before, when United had let me go, I'd thought it was all over. Managers say that telling kids they're not going to make it, is the worst part of the job.

Porterfield called me in at the end of May. I'd got three first team appearances under my belt. Things had been going well. I was expecting a decent contract. Instead, I got, 'Sorry son'. The Boss was fair about it. Told me he planned to build his team around more experienced players. Informed me that my details were being circulated. 'All the

69

best' and all that bollocks. He may as well have whacked me with a sledgehammer, then pissed in my mouth. Star of the future to no mark in five minutes.

For two weeks, I never left the house. I couldn't face my mates. Going down the dole office was something I kept putting off. Our old man said he might be able to sort me out something with him, at the steelworks. He'd been in the meeting with Porterfield. Loved it, that cunt did.

Barnsley had saved my life. Two year contract, on a fair wedge. It wasn't Real Madrid, but it was near enough. After all, Barnsley were in the Second Division. In some ways, it was a step up from the Blades. The perfect place to build my career. The team had some good players and the Boss told me he'd give me a chance. From the off, I was in and out of the firsts. By my second season, I was in more than out. I was getting established.

Right from the kick off, the pace was furious. What you'd call a typical English cup tie. Everton were as close to the perfect English side as you could get. They had it all: power, skill, organisation and ability. The speed of their passing moves was untrue. And they could mix it, when they had to. The opening ten minutes were mental. We were pumped up to get under them. Everton weren't hiding. Real blood and guts stuff.

Peter Reid picked up the ball on the right touchline. I should have been on him, but I'd been wrong footed. He was off. I had to stop him. Sharpe was in the middle. I hit

Reid so hard it was criminal. Oakwell's a tight ground; I slid in and took his legs, and the momentum of the challenge took us both crashing into the advertising boards. Crash, then a huge roar of approval. We both leapt up. Reidy was in my face. He'd every right. I gave him everything back. The other players rushed over and there was a fracas or a melee or one of those other words you only hear in football.

Basically, a bit of pushing went off. The ref had a word with the pair of us. No card, just a lame handshake. As we ran off to get in position for the free kick, I turned to him.

—That's just for starters, you Scouse cunt.

The fans could sense the aggression. The chant started.

—ANDO, ANDO.

First time I'd had my name chanted. I can't explain how good it felt. The Barnsley lads could see that I was going at it against the best and they respected me for it. Reidy smiled. He must have been a young headstrong kid, once upon a time. Peter Reid + young: a difficult concept.

The rest of the first half followed the same pattern. Any attempts at attractive, open play were stamped on mercilessly by the midfield battalions. At half-time, the match was scoreless. We were given a standing ovation (there were fuck all seats at Barnsley then). In the dressing room, Norman bellowed at us for ten minutes. Like all the other managers I played under, he subscribed to the 'It Ain't Half Hot Mum' school of motivation.

Straight after the break, the worst happened. Free kick, outside the area. Bracewell tapped it to Sheedy. Left foot. Flew into the top corner. 1-0.

Everton tightened up, but we kept going at them. The crowd responded. Football crowds will always back you up when they can see you're giving it everything. Quality and ability are optional. Effort and commitment are demanded. Fans see being a player at their club as the highest possible honour. If they could do it, they'd run themselves into the ground for the cause every week.

Of course, it's bollocks. In any group of blokes, you get sloppy cunts. A lot of the mouthiest cunts at any game spend the week being shoddy builders or skiving office bods. Put them in a team shirt and they'd be exactly the same.

That day, we were all triers. The fans couldn't fault us. Every player in red was one of them.

I suppose I was literally. By then, I'd been living in Barnsley for nearly a year; driving from my mam's every day had been too much. I was sharing a house in Athersley with Paul Greig. He was from Glasgow, but he was alright. We were both the same age and made the most of it. Plenty of lasses will do a turn for you when they find out you're a minor local celebrity.

I hardly got back to Tinsley at all. All the old lads were funny round me if I bumped into them. It was them who had the problem, not me. I went round to see Gary now and then. He'd had it rough with the strike and everything, but everyone respected him. He really believed in it. Put in more hours on union stuff on strike, than he'd put in at the pit when he was working. I don't know how he put up with that slag of a wife. If it had been up to her, he would have scabbed. Stupid cow. I mean: they had kids. I stopped slipping Gary money. He was so proud it always caused a bust up. He didn't even let me get stuff for the kids. Barbara didn't mind.

The ninety minutes were almost up. On the open kop, the scousers were starting to celebrate.

Mountfield was bringing the ball out. Oakwell was roaring for us to get into him. I went steaming at him. He knocked a lazy pass, square to Stevens.

Ronnie was on it like a whippet. Cut it off and streaked away. He looked clear. Just outside the box. Ratcliffe came out of nowhere. Ronnie had a split second. He hit it low and hard. Bottom left corner. Don't know how Southall managed to get down and push it round the post.

Everybody went up for the corner.

—BARNSLEY, BARNSLEY.

Winston placed the ball. All around him, fans were leaning over the fence. Urging, screaming, begging. I hung back, on the edge of the box. He whipped it in. Good one. Into the waiting bunch. Under pressure, Southall could only punch. The ball looped to the edge of the area. Right to me. Whack. Top corner. 1-1.

That doesn't do it justice, so let's go over the goal again, in loving, Pele in 'Escape to Victory' style, slow motion.

From Southall's fist, the ball hung for an age. I'd pulled back a step after the delivery. The ball was dropping a step to my left. Trevor Steven had been picking me up, but he'd got lost. I knew I had to hit it first time. Controlling it would be difficult and then what? Try and thread it through that mob. Impossible.

You don't go through all the options. Instinct: that's the name of the game. I threw myself at the ball. Flying scissors kick. What you might call a typical Mark Hughes strike, if he'd done it. Fortune favours the brave. Like fuck it does. Nine times out of ten, that kind of effort balloons into the crowd. 'Go on son, ave a go … you useless fuckin donkey.'

Not that day. It was my day. My 'Moment in Time'. My shot flew into the corner. Dead straight. Big Neville was out of position, but he wouldn't have got it anyway.

When it hit the net the place erupted. I turned and sprinted to the side terrace. Arms in the air. Leaping about.

Nothing can touch that feeling. Nothing.

Scoring a goal is the only time you can let it all out, when you're one of the lads. You can be yourself. Do anything. It's an outlet for any joy you've got left in your soul. For an instant, you're the man.

On the terraces, there was ecstasy. Real manly joy. A sea of hugging, kissing, shouting and clenched fists. A pile of writhing bodies developed on top of me.

I was the man.

The final whistle blew seconds after the restart. Another rush. The first person over to me was Peter Reid. He put his arms around me.

—Well done lad. Enjoy it.

A little slap on the cheek and he was off. Left me to it. What can you say about the bloke? Different class.

Me and the lads did a mini lap of honour. The fans were singing, jigging and saluting us all the way. Their gratitude was overpowering.

—BARNSLEY, BARNSLEY.

Aspirations tend to fit experience. Even then, it's hard to meet them. When you're from Barnsley, you learn not to expect too much. You daren't. Drawing at home to Everton might not seem like great; but it's better than real life.

—ANDO, ANDO.

That was sweet. I waved back. They loved it.

The party carried on in the dressing room. There was always a good atmosphere in the showers after a win, but this was something else. Lots of hugs, laughs and a full blown singalong. The block was only small, but everybody wanted to squeeze in there.

My expression must have have betrayed my smugness; the lads decided to take me down a peg or two. I felt something warm on the back of my leg. I turned to see

75

Paul, grinning like a Cheshire cat as he pissed on me.

—A golden shower for the golden boy.

A big cheer went up and all the lads surrounded me and joined in.

—You bastards.

I protested and ran out of the shower shouting, but really I thought it was as funny as the rest of them did.

There was champagne around but, as we'd not actually won, it was supposed to stay unopened. Even though I didn't mind, I had to show the lads they couldn't get away with pissing on me. You've got to be able to take it if you're going to give it out. I grabbed a bottle of bubbly and went back to the showers shaking it. I aimed, then popped it right behind Paul. The cork flew out and scored a direct hit on his arse. He let out a loud yell. Another cheer rang out. I took a long sup of the champagne that was spewing out of the bottle, then passed it to Paul. Honour had been satisfied.

I was about to get dressed when a crew from Yorkshire TV came in. Obviously, there was only one person they were interested in talking to. My interview needed seven takes; a result of my towel constantly being whipped away by team mates who were keen to increase my level of media exposure.

Afterwards, I held court in the players lounge. I fancied getting bladdered, but everyone had shit to do. Even Greig palled me out. Off out with some bird from up the road.

I couldn't get enough. I took a cab down to the Athersley Arms. It was my local, but I didn't get in there that often. When I walked in there was a murmur, then a spontaneous round of applause. It was hero worship R US all night, in there. They all wanted to be my best mate; wanted a piece of me. I just kicked back and let them. Easy to get used to that kind of thing. The best was when Match of the Day was on. I could feel everyone looking at me. Wanting to know how it felt. Wishing it was them.

I gave a knock to the offered stayback and walked home. In the morning, I bought all the papers. I went to a few different shops mind. Didn't want to look like a cocky cunt. I laid them out on the floor.

'ANDREWS RIGHT ON TIME.'

'TYKE THAT: ANDREWS LATE SHOW STUNS HOLDERS.'

Fame at last.

We lost the replay 3-0. Nobody remembers that.

QPR (h) 2nd leg

The door banged shut at ten past nine. Jackie didn't want to leave. She was always mushy and loving after a good fuck. When I'd got in the night before, she'd been upset and restless. 'We need to talk. Is there someone else?' and all that carry on.

I couldn't get my head round it after what had gone off. I shagged her hard. No prisoners; baby or no baby. At first she resisted, then she got well into it. Wild and passionate. Back to the old skool. It was the best for a long time, maybe the greatest ever. Short on style, but plenty of fortitude, dominance and impact. Jackie had cried. She was sorry about making me feel low. Everything would be alright. We loved each other and that was all that mattered. She wrapped herself round me and went to sleep with a stupid grin on her face.

It was only then that I came down. The morning after the night before. I tensed up and shuddered.

I was a murderer.

All the possible results started to shoot through my mind. It was impossible to concentrate on one for a few

79

seconds before another, more horrific scenario appeared. This went on for hours, intercut with visions of his last minutes alive.

Guilt didn't come into it. I was scared for myself. And Jackie and Annie.

In the morning, Jackie was full of the joys of spring. While she got ready for work, she kept kissing me and giving speeches on the theme of 'we're going to live happily ever after'. I played along. I knew I was going to have to get used to acting. I was desperate for her to fuck off, so I could start putting things right.

First priority was the clothes. Forensics and all that. They can pin stuff on you from one thread. I knew that I must have left some hair and skin at the scene, but there was nothing I could do about that. I had to do something. I washed all the gear I'd had on the night before. Not a word on the local news about anybody. I wanted it to keep on raining. Clean away that evidence. The clothes came out spotless; even the teeshirt. You can slag Shane Ritchie off about a lot, but the cunt knows a thing or two about washing powder.

I left the house at half ten. I dropped Annie off at the sitter's house, ('Something's come up at work, sorry about short notice, blah, blah') then drove up through Brixton.

I dumped the bag of clothes in a bin, next to the benches

across the road from the Stockwell Park estate. Later on, you always got a mob of winos hanging out there. Waterproof top, trackies, teeshirt and trainers. Gold dust; they'd go in five minutes. Only a few hundred yards from Brixton nick too. If the coppers matched some fibres, there was an outside chance they'd collar some dosser for it.

I felt pretty smart as I drove off. This wasn't a game; this was life at the limits. Stress. One false move and you're done for. Playing for high stakes brings out the best in some people. It separates the men from the boys.

I headed up to Brent Cross. It was unlikely that anyone would recognise me that far north of the river. I went to a couple of shops to replace the top, trackies and trainers. I didn't bother with the teeshirt. It was plain white. The gear I bought wasn't exactly the same, but it was near enough. No one would notice; especially not Jackie.

When I got home, I was at a loose end. What else could I do? Relax? Not in this lifetime. Not yet anyway. If it all blew over, I'd be able to deal with it. Get back to normal; whatever that means. We've all got skeletons in our cupboards, mine would be a real one. So what? I wasn't going to let it destroy me.

South London Sound. News at 2 o'clock. Item 3:
   —*A young man is in a critical condition after a savage attack in Brockwell Park. The man was discovered in the*

bushes by a council employee this morning. It is thought that he had been there overnight. Brixton police are appealing for witnesses.

He was alive. It was like a kick in the bollocks. I had nothing against the kid. I wished I'd never set eyes on him, wished that none of it had ever happened; but it had. He had to die. If he woke up, he could point the finger at me. Paul Andrews: killer, was bad, but I could beat it. The coppers would have nothing. Even if it turned to shit, it might not be the end of the world. With a good brief, I could cop for manslaughter, maybe even get off. Diminished responsibility. Temporary insanity.

MARRIED EX-PRO SNAPS WHEN CHUTNEY FERRET TAPS HIM UP.

I could say he tried to mug me.

HAVE A GO HERO FOOTBALL STAR OVERDOES RETALIATION ON THIEVING SCUMBAG.

If the bastard talked to the coppers, I was fucked. Paul Andrews: lowlife arse bandit who cruises the parks looking for rough trade.

EX-LION MAULS GAY LOVER IN MID BLOWJOB.

HOMO ANDO GIVES IT HARD WHILE PREGNANT WIFE BABYSITS.

My life would be over. Even my mam would fuck me off if it came out. Given the chance, she'd string me up.

Sit tight; that was all I could do. I managed it for fifteen minutes going on two thousand years, then stormed out.

The Sunderland trip gave me an excuse to drop in at the radio station. Going there with a dumb question about expenses would allow me to have nose in the newsroom. A chance to find out more.

Sure, it wasn't the brightest thing to do. If I lost my cool and pushed it, someone might suss. Then again, it was near where I lived. Only natural I'd be curious if someone had been croaked down the road. I didn't need much convincing.

South London Sound: the pulse of south London. One floor of a grotty tower, near the Elephant. Community broadcasting. News, sport and phone-ins. Pays the rent. Wendy on the desk confirmed the hotel's address, then I went into the news office. Tom Reed broke off from the anecdote he was boring the work experience girl with and warmly shook my hand. Good bloke Tom, though you could never really tell with journos. All those years of fake sincerity and putting punters at ease, turning the charm on and off.

I'd been buttering Tom up myself. He carried a lot of weight. You never heard him doing any of those 'down your way' community things from the radio car; unless there was a drink to be had. I'd pitched him the idea of me doing the odd studio phone-in one night down the Bell, and he hadn't dismissed the idea out of hand. Whenever I saw him, I made a point of slipping in references to current affairs. Reminding him that I knew my onions and wasn't just an 'ex-Millwall star'.

We flirted about politics for five minutes, then I went fishing.

—Anything gone off on the patch today Tom?

—Nah; just the usual. The kid in Brockwell Park look promising, but it's got no legs.

Nice one Tom. Served it up on a plate for me. No need to dig.

—What's that then?

—The parky finds a kid this morning. Kicked to shit in some bushes. Miracle he was alive. Out in the cold and rain all night. He's in Kings. Critical. It looked good till I phoned the nick. No ID, but they reckon he's a joy boy; so the story died.

—How come?

—It's going to be either local lads gay bashing or some S&M freak who went over the top. There's no angle. A kid, a pretty girl, a perky pensioner, sure. Poofters and druggies; nobody gives a shit.

—Is he going to live?

—Comatose at the moment. Odds on he'll kick it. The head injuries are consistent with a hot date with Peter Lorimer. If he makes it, he'll most likely be a cabbage. Off up to Sunderland tomorrow aren't you?

Tom set off on another of his anecdotes. I nodded and smiled as he recounted his tales of Wearside during the miner's strike. Social division, class war, violence, ravaged communities; he'd been as happy as a pig in shit. Won an award I think.

Before I went to pick up Annie, I nipped into the Charlie Chaplin for a pint, to wind down. The heat was off for the moment. Tom could spot a story and this was a non-starter. Same with the coppers probably. The hospital would have cleaned him up. Plenty of clues washed down the drain. Doctors can be wrong though. Some of these coma fellers wake up. His brain might not be as soggy as they think. In the bogs, I took out his purse. Seven quid in change, keys and a travelcard. Lee Turner. He had long hair in the picture. I'd get rid of it somewhere up the A1.

I picked Annie up on the way home. Carol wouldn't let me give her any more cash than the normal rate.

—No trouble, any time.

I was sure she fancied me. She was definitely worth one, but it wasn't worth the hassle. Jackie would find out. I stayed for a cuppa anyway.

When we got back, I started cooking dinner. Nice bit of chilli con carne. With me going away for the weekend, Jackie had been on about going out for the night, but I wasn't up to it. I was still sweating on the results from Kings.

South London Sound. News at 5 o'clock. Item 4:

—*The man found in Brockwell Park has died ...*

I hugged Annie. My destiny wasn't totally in my own hands, but it looked good. The police didn't have the same level of motivation and they had other commitments. If I didn't do anything stupid, I should be OK.

—Everything's going to be alright Annie. We're all going to live happily ever after. I went into the kitchen and threw the chilli in the bin.

—Hello Carol. I know this is takin the piss but could you ave Annie tonight? Jackie's sprung something on me. Meal out. I'd really appreciate it ...

Sheffield Wednesday (a)

—Bout six month back it were. They'd started avin rave
dos on up at t'Sal on Saturdays. Lads'd bin workin em.
Mekin a good screw an all. Anyhow, they turned up. Not
full squad, just Dixie an a few o't'others. Dancer, Tito, Nev
an that. Get to t'door and they get KB'd. Management ad
ad DS on their backs, so they'd brought in this noo door
team. All Floyds from out o town; Leeds like. Nev and that,
they've bin at it forever like. Know the score. Leave it a
week or two to settle down, then it's business as usual. So
they're shaping to fuck off, but Dixie won't ave it. Starts
gi'ing it the big un like. Y'know, like 'We run this fuckin
town. We're gunna torch this shitouse,' an all that. Off is
ead e were, badstyle. Ad a coupla digs afore e'd gone out.
All t'other lads dragged im down t'street and Tito an that
try an smarten im up, but e won't ave. Es off on one, int e.
Dixie tells em they're a set o fuckin wankers an storms back
up to t'club. They all fucked off, Dancer an that. All
carrying loadsa pills. They sussed the DS were on t'ball and
they'd be fucked if owt went off. Dixie's back up at t'door
spouting shit, but the Floyds aren't aving it. They're pro's

like. Don't wanna know. Dixie's just mekin a cunt on himsen; sayin e'll ave the lot on em. This one Floyd starts biting and Dixie's really gi'ing it to im. Billied as fuck e is. This Floyd's ad enough, so e comes out on t'street. That's summat ya never do, cos you're on yer own then. No insurance or fuck all. Fuckin schoolboy error. Dixie's bouncing round and this Floyd's laughing at im. Sorta 'Let's ave it then dickhead.' The cunts inside are lappin it up. Dixie went for it. Whips out is Stanley and slashed the Floyd. E didn't just stripe im; nearly cut the cunt in ayf. The Floyd goes isterical. Yer know. There's blood allo'er. Thinks e's gunna die. In shock like. All t'others pile out an it it's Dixie like. Ya know. Big, fuck off rush o super reality. So e's on is toes. Away. Anyway, e oled up at is flat forra coupla days. Shittin it e were. Ya know what the Floyds are like. Sort out their own shit. No fuckin coppers or owt like that. E phoned me up an telled me e were fuckin off to India, but is ead were shot to fuck. Cunt get it together to go out to t'shop, ne' mind fuckin India. E were oled up for four days afore they come round. Dawn raid. Lucky for im the coppers got im first. The Floyd who e carved up weren't the real deal, just some student wi a thick neck earning pocket money. Coughed the lot in ospital; statement, the works. The coppers turned Dixie's place upside down, but they only found a bit o grass an about an arf an ounce o wiz. Nowt worth bothering wi. E got remanded in Armley. They were tryin for attempted murder for starters but dropped it

88

to malicious wounding. Three year. Enough for them cos e ad a two year bender on im from that factory thing. E's up in Frankland. Fuckin grown up time ya do up there. No messin. Like it or not e'll get smartened up. Should be out in another two, if e keeps is ead down. Daft cunt.

Chip stared straight ahead at the road. His stammer was history. All the time he'd been recounting the ballad of Carl Dixon, he'd not shown a flicker of emotion. He just reeled off the story, like he was telling me about the video he watched last night, not how his (former?) closest friend was doing a five in a maximum security prison for almost killing a man.

The two guys in the back had their fourpenneth.

—Using an dealin. Just askin forrit.

—Oistin were Dixie's game. E shoulda stuck to that. E'll be alright though. Might do im some good.

Classic lad understatement. Business and pleasure don't mix, stick to what you know, he'll survive. Attempted murder, prison, drug dealing. Just a typical day at the office, dear.

I didn't know the lads in the back, but they looked heavy duty. They were mates of Chip. He'd introduced them as Bernie and Tosh. I was sure they knew who I was, but they never let on. Hard bastards never do. They're used to being the centre of attention. They demand it. I tried to keep the conversation going, to show I knew the score as much as anything.

—If ya mess about wi that shit, yer always gunna get it in the end.

There was an embarrassed silence in the car. I could tell they all knew that I didn't have a clue what I was on about.

I felt like a young virgin, discussing sex with lads who'd 'done it'. Weird it was. I was the successful bloke, the well paid local celeb, but in this company I was the runt. No form plus no reputation for scuffling equals no credibility. It was such a contrast to the night before. My first taste of glory since I'd been back at the Blades.

WOLVERHAMPTON WANDERERS 2
SHEFFIELD UNITED 2

We'd both needed a draw to be promoted to the Second. Mathematically, Port Vale could still push us into the play offs, if they ran up a cricket score in their last match and we got gubbed at Bristol City, but that was, as they say, of academic interest only.

Man, it had been fantastic. The highlight of my career to then. The fans knew we were on the verge of something. You don't know what it's like to get that kind of acclaim.

The Blades had been waiting long enough. Porterfield had taken them up the year he let me go, but they got stuck. His 'Dads Army' ran out of steam and he got the boot after three years of Second Division under achievement. McEwan took over and went too far the other way; all kids. He'd been fired halfway through the season and Dave Bassett was selected as his replacement. Old 'Dirty Harry' himself. Too late to keep them up though.

At the beginning of the 88/89 season, Harry was looking to rebuild the United side. He needed quality players with a bit of fight in them. Lads who could handle the rough stuff. You needed a bit of that to get out of the Third. £200,000 he paid for me.

Sure I felt smug. I'd been let go for fuck all. I'd proved a few people wrong. Five good years I'd had at Barnsley. From no-mark to first team regular. My game had really come on with the Tykes. Midfield anchor who popped up with a few goals a season. Sort of a poor man's Steve MacMahon. I knew it was time to move though.

At the press conference and in the interviews, I gave everybody what they wanted: 'How I loved United. The move was a dream come true,' etc.

All total bollocks. Harry came up with more cash than I was on at Barnsley. Simple as that. Footballers are the same as anyone else. If you get offered more money for doing the same job, you move.

Course, there were fringe benefits. Nicer facilities and bigger crowds to fan the ego with. Also, United had more potential. Fellers like Bassett bring a buzz with them. The way I saw it, Barnsley were stuck. Midtable Second Division: 1981—hell freezing over. The Blades were in the Third, but you could see better things on the horizon.

Better results, better crowds, better bonuses.

Footballwise, everything went to plan. We were in the top three all season, battling it out with Wolves and Vale. On a personal level, I'd say my performances more than justified the fee.

I could have carried on living in Athersley, but I'd got a bit pissed off with it since Paul Greig left. He moved to Bury for £25,000. He commuted at first, then he met some bird over there. Saddled with a mortgage, a fat Lancashire tart and playing at Gigg Lane. Pity. He was a sound lad Paul.

I moved to Brinsworth. Rented a semi there. Nice area it is. Just over the border, in Rotherham. It was only about two miles from my mam's place in Tinsley, but I never used to go up there. Well only to pick up my mam, to bring her round to mine every now and then.

Loved coming round she did. She was really proud. Posh house; garden and everything. Pissed our old man off too. She was always telling me I should buy it. She didn't get it.

In my time at Barnsley, I'd lost touch with all my old mates. I didn't bother putting that right when I moved back. Most of the time I hung around with lads from the club, although I did drink at the local in Brinsworth quite a lot. Plenty of Blades got in there, so I used to get the royal treatment.

In fact, I got quite into the respectable, suburban bit. Driving myself to training every day. Nice easy run it was, down the Parkway. I even had the odd round of golf, for fuck's sake.

Almost as soon as I arrived in Brinny, I started seeing Michelle. She was a decent bird by any measure. Good looking and she had a pretty high up job at the Nat West, even though she was only my age. Apart from her constant financial advice, we got on great. By the end of the season, we were practically living together at mine.

It was when I was out with Michelle one night that I bumped into Chip. We'd been for an Indian down Rotherham, just after Christmas, and decided to go on to a club.

When we got there, Chip was on the door. I'd never had much time for Chip. Always seen him as a big, thick cunt who nobody would give the time of day if he wasn't a hard bastard. Dixie's ferocious poodle. Funny though, that night I ended up chatting to him quite a bit. Not out of charity or fear but because he was alright. He'd changed since we were younger. I suppose we all do. He seemed a lot more on the ball.

After that, Chip phoned me up a couple of times about going out for a drink. I knocked him back both nights. Had a promotion push to concentrate on, didn't I?

At the the end of February, he called again with a very tempting offer:

Wednesday 10th May
Royal Albert Hall
The Middleweight Championship of the World
MIKE 'THE BODYSNATCHER' MACALLAM
(Champion, Jamaica)
V
HEROL 'BOMBER' GRAHAM
(Challenger, Sheffield)

Chip, in common with most hard bastards, had tried his hand at boxing as a lad. By all accounts he wasn't half bad either. To cut a long story short (like I wish Chip had had the fucking sense to), he used to train at Brendan Ingle's gym over in Wincobank, same as Bomber Graham. Chip had been on the blower to a bloke who knew a bloke and he'd got four comps. Not quite ringside but not that far off. Did I fancy it?

That ranked as one of the most stupid fucking questions that Chip had ever asked. Trouble was, the fight was bang in the middle of the last week of the season. For a minute I wished I had a regular job. One where you can knock a sickie if you've got something better to do.

I laid it out for Chip. I'd only be able to go if we were up already. If not, the Gaffer would definitely have us in for training the day after the Wolves game. Chip said he'd put one by for me, just in case. More than sporting I'd say. We'd made it by the skin of our teeth, so there I was.

It was about two by the time we hit London. Chip said we'd be best off going for a pint round Gloucester Road and found his way there pretty easily.

He was emerging as a bit of a dark horse old Chip. On the road down, I'd been thinking I'd made a mistake. It had been all fighting and crime talk. Like schoolkids, only for higher stakes. Once we got in the boozer, everything lightened up.

The ale was going down well. I'd meant to take it easy, what with training the day after and the trip to Bristol on the Friday, but that soon went out of the window. Fuck it. With a clean run home after the fight, I'd be in bed for three. I'd been on the piss later than that before and managed to get away with it.

I never got round to asking Chip what he was up to. He was shacked up with some bird in Clifton and bouncing, but that was obviously only half the story.

The cunt was loaded. Armani from head to foot and the motor was brand new. I didn't push it. I remembered some of the old ways at least.

I always enjoyed going to London. It wasn't the hicky Northern thing about the day out in the 'Big Smoke'. There was just something I liked about the place. Couldn't really put my finger on it. Chip was well up for it. He was obviously the main man of the team. Tosh and Bernie were careful round him.

You could tell it was more than just his capacity for head

busting that gave him rank. The man himself was on top form, lecturing his two oppos on the details of my career. A few pints down the line, we got on to the inevitable: 'Whatever Happened to the Likely Lads?'

Dixie was accounted for. In the pub, Chip muttered that Dixie was a cheap piece of shit. The other two nodded agreement. I had no idea what had gone off, but one thing was for sure. Nobody took Chip for a big dozy twat any more.

Chip said Hastey was still living at home. Working with his old man. Plumber's mate. Still dipping his mam's purse too. Gary had dropped off the face of the Earth. Word was he'd moved to Maltby pit and bought a shitty little semi up there. Spent all his time on political bollocks and looking after the kids. Chip told me he'd seen Barbara round town with other fellers. I'd seen that coming a mile off.

We hit four or five boozers round Gloucester Road and South Ken. From about 4pm, it started to fill up with Sheffield lads down for the fight. I started to get plenty of backslaps from the Blades present. I gladly accepted their thanks, on behalf of all the players, management and coaching staff. Some Pigs gave me shit too, but it was all good natured.

Course that didn't last. The pub we were in got mobbed out with Blades. Quite a few top lads in. Even I could spot some, from the old days. There was a smattering of Pigs but they were all 'genuine fans', so they were tolerated.

Everything changed at half six. The door opened and five blokes came in. Identikit bad lads: dressed to the nines, but rough round the edges. The mood in the pub changed immediately. Banter was a thing of the past. These weren't just Pigs, they were top Pigs. Straight away they sussed the situation and fucked off. A token force chased out after them. Everyone laughed about it.

—Set of wankers blah blah.

Two hundred on to five. They're nice odds to have.

Ten minutes later.

CRRRAAASSHH!

The windows went. Bricks, rocks, the fucking lot. Glass flying everywhere. Outside there's a few chants of OCS. Inside every fucker's ducking for cover. Total panic. It went quiet for a couple of seconds. Then it was counter attack time. The place emptied. A huge scrum desperately cramming through the narrow door, all eager to feast on Pig. I scanned round. The pub looked like a Greek wedding in Beirut. A few bloody casualties littered the place and that was it. Everyone else was on the street trying to kick off a mini-riot. Everyone except me, Chip, Tosh and Bernie.

During the bombardment we'd been by the bar, away from the danger zone. Bernie had set off to join the Blades storming out after the Pigs, but Chip had grabbed him.

—Leave it Bern. Fuck all to do wi us.

Pissed as I was, I knew not to go outside. I couldn't in my position; even if I'd wanted to. Chip finished his pint.

—Best we get round to t'Albert Hall. We'll not get another ere now.

Wise words indeed.

Boxing—*the Sportsman's View*:

The Noble Art. The ultimate sport. Two finely tuned athletes, in the peak of physical condition, battle for the spoils. No days off allowed. No putting it right next Saturday. No getting carried by your team mates. Skill, power, aggression, mental toughness, speed, agility, timing, bravery. The ultimate sport.

Boxing—*The Lad's View*:

The ultimate bloke sport. Only place you can be guaranteed a proper ruck. Roll up and see fit blokes really give it to each other. Blood and guts on demand.

It was the first time I'd ever been to the Albert Hall. Impressive, the only word for it. The place was about a third full for the undercard. All six-rounders featuring Barney Eastwood proteges wiping the floor with anonymous foreigners. I was glad that Chip and the boys were straight up boxing fans. Keeping up with them had been a struggle. I did most of my supping with other players. We all kidded ourselves, but we weren't really big drinkers. It's impossible if you want to maintain any level of fitness. Going out with real lads had brought it home— with a bang. First time I'd gone over a gallon for yonks. A couple more and I'd have been out for the count.

The main event came round quick enough.

MIKE MACALLUM V BOMBER GRAHAM

People could relate to Bomber. Sheffield lad. Never got his shot earlier because he wouldn't move to London. Everyone was scared of him, too talented. Yeah. South Yorkshire folk would listen to that all day. Nearly true as well. Except he'd blown his big chance two years before against Kalambay. And the reason nobody wanted to put him on in London was because he didn't sell tickets. He had all the moves, Ron Atkinson would probably describe him as a fanny merchant. Trouble was, he didn't bang. Joe Public wants blood. Brutality puts bums on seats.

Truth be told, the Sheffield lads would've preferred it if Bomber had been an animal. Less technical, more deadly. Their perfect fighter would be a whiter brawler who clubbed the opposition to sleep. Still, you've got to be grateful for what you've got. So he's a bit of a ponce, he's a local lad, got to get behind him.

The fight went the distance. Technically excellent defensive challenger versus wily, experienced old champion. Never going to be anything else, was it?

Not much to get the crowd excited. Odd atmosphere it was. Some singing and chanting from the lads in the cheap seats up the top, but it lacked passion. Like it was something they didn't really believe in. Not like football.

A few times, everyone's eyes turned away from the ring as tell-tale gaps appeared in the crowd. Minor scuffles. Blades and Pigs: work and drink together every day of the week without a sniff of bother. Stick them at a sporting event and they'll start knocking lumps out of each other.

Naturally everyone went barmy at the decision. Majority verdict for the champion. Graham had had a point docked for holding. It would have been enough to tilt it his way. Perfect ending for Sheffield fans. Glorious defeat.

We got off straight away. I was relieved. I'd had visions of being in a club till the early hours and fuck knows what else after that. As it stood I'd be in a state the following morning. I reckoned the boss would go easy. We were all up after all.

I couldn't believe Chip. He'd been supping all day but he seemed stone cold. Unreal. He didn't think twice about driving home. I was cabbaged. Just settled down and tried to get some kip. We'd had a decent crack. Right enough the trip home was going to be a bit of a bind and the fight had been a crock of shit but, all in all, I was quite pleased I'd turned out. It was the 'I was there' factor. To have lived a full life, there are a few things you've got experience. I could put a tick next to: attend a world title fight. For a while, the others traded cliches they'd nicked from Reg Gutteridge.

—A challenger's got to come out and win t'title. Matchin

t'champs not good enough.

—Occasion got to im.

—Trains too ard. Left is fight in t'gym.

Time was dragging. I fell asleep.

—Ere y'are Paul. Let's be avin ya.

At first, I thought we were home. A look out of the window dashed my hopes.

Motorway services. Leicester Forest.

It was about half two and I felt pretty rough. To be honest, I fancied staying in the car and crashing out, but it wasn't on. The others were into having a laugh, so I got dragged along.

Naturally, the bogs were first on the agenda, then a quick scout round. Everything was shut bar a restaurant type joint and a mini amusement arcade. Chip and Tosh were well up for it. Piled wads of cash into one of them Kung Fu games. Doing my head in they were, them two screaming and shouting while they kicked fuck out of each other on the screen, with Bernie doing a manic commentary.

I fucked off to the cafe, to get a bit of peace. I was on my own in there for about ten minutes, nursing a pot of tea. Some little manager bloke was hassling the lass on the till, making her clean everything while it was slow. We were only an hour or so from home and I wanted those cunts to get a move on so I could have my bed.

I heard the lads come in. About fucking time. I turned round. Wrong people. Totally wrong fucking people. The Sheffield accents belonged to a group of five lads. I clocked them straight away. Bad lads. The Pigs who'd kicked everything off at the pub earlier. I was very sober all of a sudden.

Right away I knew how bad it could get. I hoped they wouldn't clock me, but there was fuck all chance of that. They were full time lads. Scanning the place when they walked in. We're the boys, what of it?

Four of them went up to the counter, but one walked round to get a table. I could feel him giving me the deadeye. I stared deep into my empty cup. He stopped next to me, stared hard, then walked back to the others. I glanced up. They'd sussed me.

The five of them came strolling over and stood round the table. This shit wasn't going to blow over. I looked up. I could see in their eyes that I wasn't going to get away with this. Total humiliation was the best I could hope for.

In the middle was a big cunt. Definitely the top lad. Big, fat cunt with long, permed hair and a Burberry jacket. I thought my best shot was trying to calm it down.

—Alright lads. Bin to the fight?

—Fuck off Pig.

The fat bastard spat it out. The others didn't laugh. They meant business. Something was holding them back. I don't know what. They wanted me, no doubt on that score, but

102

none of them wanted to make the first move. Lads code? Five to one's not on. The fact I was a player? Players never get whacked.

—Look lads. I don't want no trouble.

—I'm gunna brek yer fuckin legs Andrews.

To get to the door, I'd have to go straight through them. I was more frightened than I'd ever been in my life. Fuck it. I was going to get done. I'd go down like a lad. I stood up. This took them back a bit. They were expecting me to swallow and wait for them to piss on me. I'd got them off guard. Charge and I might make the door. The fat cunt was first to switch back on. He starts bouncing a little. Coming towards me, hands down. I didn't want to back off, but I couldn't help it.

—PAUL!

Chip shouting made him hesitate for a split second. I dived at the fat cunt. Didn't punch him, more barged him over a table.

The other Pigs were bouncing. Caught in two minds. Take care of me or get the fuck away from the cavalry.

Chip and the other lads were flying over the tables. These cunts were ours. I made it hard for the one nearest to me. Skinny, young un.

—Come on Pig. Let's ave it then.

He moves forward a bit, then thinks better of it. I turn and get whacked up the side of my head. The fat, curly bastard's back up and he's fucking game. The cunt's just shaping to fuck me up when Chip arrives. Takes him round the neck. Crashes into the table. Chip holds him down and starts laying into the cunt. Blood flying all over every time his fist thuds into his face. I run over.

—Gunna brek my legs are ya? Ya fuckin Pig.

As I finished I kicked him hard in the bollocks. Mr Top Banana Wednesday fan was wasted. Cunt'll be walking like Tina Turner for a while too.

Me and Chip spun round. Bernie was wrestling with a Pig, on the floor. We ran over and stomped the cunt till he let go. Bernie stood up, booted the cunt, then spat on him. We could hear some shouting outside. The three of us piled out. Tosh had a Pig walled up. The bastard's dial bashed up to fuck. He was out on his feet. Tosh was screaming at him giving him the head.

—Fuck about with my mates, eh?

Head.

—Ard man, eh?

Head.

He saw us and let go of the Pig. The cunt crumpled to the ground. Tosh and Chip sorted out the business.

—Where's the others?

—On their toes. Fuckin wankers. Who were they?

—OCS.

—Who?

Tosh was a Rotherham lad and not much of a football fan. He'd steamed in because that's what you do.

—Wednesday.

—Good. I ate them cunts.

We all smiled.

—Come on. Let's fuck off.

Aston Villa (h) FA Cup 4th Round

The Sunday night drive home down the M1 was fucking murder. I mean, fair enough, I'm not the greatest driver in the world but at least I've got half an ounce of common sense. The way some of the cunts weave about. And in weather like that.

I had no reason to rush home, as Jackie had taken Annie to her parents' place for a couple of nights to avoid being at home alone. I could have stayed another night in Sheffield but there was no point. Once you've been away for a bit you end up a stranger in your own town. That had bothered me at first, but not any more. I bet that some of the lads I was at school with, who took the straight road, talk to our old man in the club now. If it's a choice between that and being an outsider—no contest.

By the time I passed the Nottingham turn off, the number of cars on the motorway was getting dangerous. I pulled in at Trowell services for a cuppa. The journey home was going to be like the rest of the day. A fucking nightmare.

★

The drive up the day before had been OK. Wads of slush and shit, but that was alright. Kept the traffic down. I didn't mind taking it slow anyway. In my head I was away: France 98, I'd prefer Japan in 2002, but South Korea would do. They'd called me on Thursday, Radio 5.

—Would you be interested in being our summariser at Bramall Lane on Sunday? ... We feel that as an ex-Blade blah blah ... own place in Cup folklore blah blah ... impressed by your work with South London Sound blah blah.

It was like getting an international call-up. Not that I bought the flannel. It was obvious that somebody had dropped them in the shit at the last minute, but so what? It doesn't matter how you get your chance, it's how you perform. Look at Geoff Hurst in 66.

I'd stayed at the Grosvenor, with 5 Live picking up the bill. They weren't usually that generous but, short notice etc. Couple of beers in the bar then early to bed. I wanted to be fresh for the match.

I'd headed up to the Lane at one. Four o'clock kick off, so I had three hours of hanging about doing broadcast stuff. Brown-nosing really. When your job is commenting on incidents in the game, there's only a limited amount of prep you can do.

I hardly knew anyone at the club any more. I did manage to grab a word with Howard Kendall. Naturally he made a crack about the equaliser in 85. At the time he said it was one of the best strikes he'd ever seen. Nice bloke Howard, he deserves any success he gets with the Blades. Especially after all that Notts County bollocks.

Villa were the form team in the land. The Blades were on the up since Howard took over. Dumped Arsenal out in the Third round after a replay. It was all set up. The kind of tie the FA Cup's all about. Premier League high flyers away to Second Division, sorry First Division, battlers. The nation was hungry for it. To be honest, the nation had no choice, it was the only game of any merit to beat the shitty weather that weekend and it was the live game on BBC 1. The nation expected a classic:

SHEFFIELD UNITED 0 ASTON VILLA 1

The match was everything that someone who's been to the Lane as often as me should have expected. Shit game, disappointing atmosphere, away win. I don't know. I suppose I thought that if the game was exciting, people would remember it and I'd get some reflected glory. Guilt by association. If you saw it on telly, you'll know it was one of the most boring games in history. Official.

That's where I fucked up, I was over eager. Too keen to make a good impression. Since Sky started doing all the football, they're way over the top: Andy Gray coming in his boxers over nil-nils at The Dell. As a reaction, all your 5 Live bods are a lot more chilled out: if a game's crap, they admit it, then start bullshitting about whatever, like the cricket dudes always have.

All through the match they were just kicking it. Then it's over to me and I'm going off on one. Talking about the systems and who's in what role and how fascinating the tactical battle is—I must have sounded like Alan Green's trainspotter cousin. Fucking nightmare.

I might have been a bit hard on myself. I felt as though I'd had a shot and fucked it up bigtime. Geoff Thomas proportions.

All the commentators said I'd done alright when we had a drink after, it was their looks I didn't like. Those 'Get real you has-been' looks. If I'd told Jackie or anyone, they'd have said I was imagining it. Course they would. They'd never been anybody. They didn't know the other look. Still, no point dwelling on it after the event.

I finished the last of my cold tea. It was time to get back on the road. The service area was full of nobodies. I realised that being anonymous was a lot less difficult than it used to be.

If anything, it was even colder when I got back to the Mondeo. Eight o'clock. Even at a snail's pace I'd be in the house before midnight. I slowly drove out of the car park, on to the slip road. That's when I saw him. Young lad. I'd guess late teens. Hitching in that weather. I pulled up and he came steaming over.

—Where ya goin?

—London.

—It's yer lucky night.

The kid got in and threw his bag on to the back seat. One of them little Head bags. He was wearing some kind of navy, canvas cagoule style top, Adidas ski hat, decent jeans and a pair of Vans. Not bad. He'd have to answer a few Style Patrol questions but Normski would definitely let him off. He looked a normal kid. One of the lads.

—What's yer name?

—Tony.

—I'm Paul.

—Come far today Tony?

—Leeds.

—What's in London?

—Mates.

That was about it for my attempts at conversation. The kid just mumbled. Didn't want to know. I told him where I'd been and that I was an ex-pro. I was getting a few things off my chest really. And I suppose I was showing off a bit. He seemed fairly impressed. Hard to tell though. Dead quiet he was, Tone.

My monologue tapered off. I could relate to the way he was acting. I hate cunts who go on about themselves all the time. Smug bastards. They aren't really interested in you. The only reason they chat is to let you know how well they're doing or to see what you can do for them.

It went ultra-quiet. I stuck on one of Jackie's mix tapes, Paul Oakenfold I think. In a way, I suppose I chose that one to make me look good, show the lad I was still on the cutting edge. Bit sad when you think about it.

I started to mull over my future. Or, more truthfully, I started wallowing in depression. The Radio 5 gig was in ruins. My glittering media career looked pretty much in the toilet. For months I'd been thinking that something would turn up. It had, and I'd fucked it up.

What now?

Jackie's old man had been pitching a few ideas; through Jackie of course. He could sort me out with something with one of his builder buddies. He'd love that, the cunt. Having me as a lackey. Paying his daughter's bills and having me in his debt. Jackie was five months gone. Time was running out. Accepting defeat and a life in Stiffsville would be bad enough, but having to thank that twat for anything. Fuck's sake. I couldn't think of anything worse.

Straight away, I thought of something worse. Life imprisonment for a brutal murder. Sex crime. I might have to do my time on the beast wing. Shame, disgrace. No visits. On my guard 24:7:365.

Having something like that hanging over you helps to keep things in perspective. At first I'd been a wreck. Every time the doorbell went, I thought the game was up. You've never seen a pair of Jehovah's Witnesses welcomed so warmly. I couldn't do anything. And I mean anything.

Paranoia and North Sea prick. It was like a never ending speed comedown.

It says a lot about how things were between me and Jackie, that she didn't notice any difference at first. Then it was, 'We've got to talk ... whatever it is, you can tell me.' She thought I was hiding an affair and/or a coke habit. If only. I told her I was depressed over how the work situation was shaping up and all that. Jackie bought it. I felt insulted that she thought I was such a sad cunt I'd get that messed up about petty shit. Occasionally, I thought about telling her the truth. Those impulses usually lasted around half a second.

For a few weeks Jackie mothered me; she was good at that. By the middle of January, we even managed sex a couple of times a week. It was a great relief. Made Jackie happy and stopped her from asking questions.

The state of play in the Lee Turner investigation probably had a lot to do with the resumption of 'normal' marital relations. Tom Reed's nose for a story had been as reliable as ever. In a violent world, 'Faggot Battered to Death in Park' runs for about as long as Brian Marwood's England career.

One of the lads at South London Sound knew a cop at Brixton nick; they had fuck all. The CID were working on some sadist boyfriend theory/fantasy. Not that they were breaking their backs on it. There had been a whisper that a group of activists were looking to use the case to highlight homophobia in general. As far as I was aware, that had come to nothing.

As I saw it, I was in the clear. The trail was cold. My biggest worry had been forensics. If there were any witnesses I would have been long nicked. They would have at least issued a description. I figured I must be out of the woods.

I knew I'd never really be free again. Lee Turner. How many times had I seen his face? Looking down at his dead body. He wasn't dead until the day after, but I knew he'd not get up again.

Two months had gone by since. That meant I'd been over it a few million times. Why did I go back around the park? Why did I stop? Why did I let him do that to me?

I wished I'd never set eyes on him, but I had. What was important was to stop any more damage. If I could, I'd have confessed, but who would that have helped? He'd still be dead. His family? What satisfaction would they get from another life being ended? Besides, I had a family. Jackie, Annie and the one on the way. My mam. For their sakes I'd have to suffer with this forever. It wasn't all about self-preservation.

Nothing like a little soul searching to pass the time.

Tony stared straight ahead. Barrel of laughs these Leeds kids. We passed Toddington services. Less than an hour to go. Jackie's old man had brought a bottle of Glenfiddich round at Christmas. This was definitely the night to make a dent in it.

I glanced at Tony through the corner of my eye. He wasn't the world's greatest conversationalist, but he seemed alright. I decided to do him a favour.

—Where yer stayin in London, Tone?

He just mumbled something along the lines of 'don't know'. I reckoned I'd just caught him napping. We hadn't said a word to each other for two hours. I tried again.

—It'll be fucking murder for ya gettin across town at this time on a Sunday. If ya tell me where the mates yer stoppin wi live, I'll drop ya near there.

—I ant got no mates.

—Eh?

—I ant got no mates.

I didn't get it. I was trying to help the lad out and he was getting all moody. All I wanted was to get home. I didn't need this shit. I've got a baby at home if I fancy a game of silly cunts.

I suppose it was because of that I pushed it. My paternalistic instincts. You get a nose for when something's up. He was a Yorkshire lad, dressed to the nines and giving it the 'who the fuck are you' bit; but his heart wasn't in it. Last chance Tone lad.

—Where you stopping tonight?

That opened Selwyn Froggat's cupboard. Everything fell

out. He started shaking, then blubbing. Just a little at first, then the full Alex Higgins. Lads crying. Man it got to me. Usually I couldn't even bear to look.

This was different, though. I felt for the kid. I didn't know him—I'd hardly got two words out of him all night—but I knew his type. For a lad like him to crack it must be bad scenes at Jangles. I wanted to put my arm round him. Not like that. It's just, when you're in the shit, people always say they know how you feel, when really they know fuck all. Thing is; whatever shit he was in, I was going through worse. I could handle it—that's all.

It sounds daft, but I think he could sense it. He let go. We weren't driver and hitcher any more, we were shrink and patient. He could tell I cared. I envied him.

There weren't any mates in London. He had to get away from his life in Leeds. I got the edited lowlights. Tony was eighteen; fresh out of a kids' home. He didn't say too much about the place, just that there'd been abuse. I had to read between the lines.

Anyway, he'd been fostered. Seemed a nice family at first, then it fucked up. Tony's foster dad started shagging him. He reckoned the mother knew as well. He got sent back to the home, and more of the same. He'd finally left the home a few months before, and within a fortnight they'd been round, all the scum from his past. All wanting the same. Poor bastard.

He just sat there when he'd got it all out. I say all, but

I'm sure there was more; from what you hear about these things, there's always more. Drugs, rent, glue, suicide attempts and whatever. I could smell the shame oozing from him. Relieved, but wishing he'd kept his gob shut.

He looked as sheepish as you can without actually saying baa. All he could see was me from the outside: Sheffield lad made good. How could I understand with my townie mentality? 'Why dint you stand up to em? Nob'dy'd ever punch mah fuckin doughnut.' How wrong he was. A few years back, maybe, but I'd seen through all that. I was as much a victim as he was.

I put away nearly half of the bottle of malt when I got home. In the dark—no lights, no music, nothing.

Tony was upstairs, asleep in the spare room. I had to put him up after all that. Least I could do. Besides, it was freezing outside. It didn't matter how good the whisky was, it still made me feel queasy. Spirits never agree with me, but I carried on regardless. I was thinking about what had become of me. Far too painful to do sober.

I thought I'd got a grip on things until I'd picked up Tony. He'd brought it on again. Tony: normal, working class Yorkshire lad. What did he have to look forward to? No job, no home, no family. He'd end up like the other runaways—on the meat rack, getting fucked by fat businessmen then dying. It's all he knew. Being used. Being screwed.

What about me? What excuse did I have? Normal life. Mam and Dad. Wife and kid. Why had I gone into the bushes with that kid?

No. It wasn't the park thing that was really eating me. It was Tony. When I picked him up, did I have something else on my mind? Subconscious like. I didn't know. When he'd opened up I'd felt for him. What was it? Sympathy? Consolation? Lust?

He was asleep upstairs. I could picture him—in bed, naked. I could just walk in and fuck him. When I offered him a bed, he probably thought that's what I meant. What he's used to. He expected it. Nobody had forced him to come. He wanted me.

I finished my glass. God it burned.

Tony got off at about ten the morning after. I bunged him fifty quid. It was all the cash I had in the house. Where he went, I've got no idea. Not my problem. That may sound heartless but what can you do? It's his life. I feel sorry for the kids in Ethiopia, but I can't put them up either.

I set about clearing the house up, ready for Jackie and Annie getting back. As it goes, I felt pretty good about life for a change. It was the look Tony had given me when he'd left. Everyone who'd ever done anything for him had expected something in return. Not me. I'd given him a lift, put him up, heard his confession and slipped him a few quid on his way out. He respected me.

I couldn't wait to see Annie. She always went nuts when she hadn't seen Daddy for a few days. Big hugs all round. Work was dodgy and there was the other stuff, but the important things were still in place. Tony. I could have done anything to him. He wanted me to, but I didn't. I thought about it, sure. Everyone fantasises. That's normal. Anyway, that was the whisky more than anything. When it came down to it, I didn't want to know. The park had been a one-off.

I nipped to the shops to get a surprise for Annie.

13th May 1989

Bristol City (a)

The coppers pulled us about ten minutes up the road from the services.

We were kept hanging about for another twenty five before the van came to take us back to Leicester nick. Chip kept winking at me. Keeping me on the straight and narrow.

I'd not been banged up since I was at school, for lifting tapes at Debenhams. I was pretty cool about it though. Things could have panned out a lot worse. If the lads hadn't arrived I'd have been history. We'd be alright. The manager guy would fill them in. Self defence. Being pissed helped me to keep things in perspective.

Once the coppers had found out I was a footballer with no form, they were sound. A bit patronising and sarcastic, but that's in their nature. Apparently, one of the Pigs was in hospital. They interviewed the four of us, but nobody said fuck all. I even managed to get some kip in the cell. When they found out the Pig wasn't seriously hurt, they sprung us. Bailed to report back in four weeks. Didn't even breathalyze Chip.

It was six o'clock when we got back on the road. Everybody was giddy. Same as on the way down, only this time I was part of it. Sitting in a cell was old hat to those lads. Me, I'd done everything by the book. Stood my ground, got stuck in and kept my gob shut. I was alright: official.

The consensus was that nothing would come of it. The caff manager would tell them who started it. The coppers didn't give a fuck. They only got shit when local crime wasn't cleared up. A mob of mental Yorkies knocking lumps out of each other at the services didn't interest them. Waste of resources.

The day after, I told Bassett everything.

I was late for training and fucked. Besides, I reckoned he'd find out in the end anyway, so being (nearly) straight about it was the best policy.

That was a good call. He got phoned up by a journo after a quote, while I was still in his office. He wasn't best pleased about me being out and pissed at that time of night, let alone the brawling and getting nicked part. Still, Bassett will always stick by you if you're alright with him. I mean, it wasn't as if I'd gone looking for it. He fined me a week's wages and promised he'd look after me if the blokes upstairs kicked off.

It got a decent spread in the Star that night.

BLADES STAR IN POLICE QUIZ

United midfielder Paul Andrews was arrested last night in connection with a brawl at a motorway service station. Violence erupted at Leicester Forest as Blades and Owls fans clashed on the way home from Bomber Graham's unsuccessful world title challenge. Two men, believed to be Wednesdayites, were taken to hospital. Restaurant manager Shabir Akthar said: 'They were like wild animals. There was blood everywhere.'

Leicester police confirmed that Andrews had been arrested, but no decision had been made about whether he would be charged with an offence. Andrews was unavailable for comment. Blades boss Dave Bassett said he would be speaking to the player.

We travelled to Bristol on the Friday. Stayed in Weston-Super-Mare overnight.

The hotel had been booked well in advance, back when it looked like a do or die job. It looked a bit extravagant, but I think we'd earned it really. The Boss made me sub, because of all the shit flying about the services thing. I had no problem with that. In the circumstances, I was grateful for a place on the bench.

Running out at Ashton Gate was fantastic. Bright sunshine. Thousands of ecstatic Blades. Total party atmosphere. We got a massive ovation from the travelling support. The fans always used to chant a few of the player's names while we were warming up. Always Deano first, then Tony Agana. Quite right too. Top players. The lads who got all our goals.

That day was different. As soon as they'd done singing 'United', all the Blades started at once.

—ANDO, ANDO, ANDO.

Instead of waving to acknowledge them, I clenched my fists, screwed up my face and did a bit of shadow boxing. You've never heard a cheer like it in your fucking life. The Bristol City game will always stay with me because of that. I didn't even get on, and we got beaten, but every time I did a jog down the line, the fans were going berserk for me.

I'd been dead lucky at the services. Years later, I'd wake up sweating, thinking about how bad it could have got. About how much shit I'd have taken before I'd have had a go on my own. It worked out fine for me. I'd actually done very little, everything had been down to Chip, Tosh and Bernie: the real hard men. Not according to the stories that got round though; made me sound like Jean Claude Van Damme and Mike Tyson rolled into one.

The fans loved me.

I mean they really loved me. If you're a good player, who does well for the team, they like you. I was that, but the Leicester Forest gig gave me much more. Put me on a whole higher plane. 'Pigs hospitalised by pissed up Blades player.'

Unprecedented street cred. Add that I was from Sheffield
and grew up a Blade.

I was the perfect local hero.

Fuck Bomber Graham.

Charlton Athletic (a)

—Thirty seconds.

I took a deep breath.

—Are you OK Paul?

—No problem. I've had forty thousand people boo me before.

—Forty thousand. If only.

I laughed and my producer, Charlotte, gave me a hopeful smile back. Didn't exactly inspire confidence our Charlie. Like all media types, she applied the Shankly school of philosophy to her job. Sometimes I had to take a step back to avoid getting caught up in it. In the real world, what did it matter if some crappy radio show went wrong?

I was shitting myself, but not about the show itself— more the subject matter.

My opponent was in a state. Outwardly he looked alright. Early twenties, bit lanky, with tidy, side parted hair and a tweedy suit on. His body language gave him away though. Anxious and lacking confidence. His first time on air.

I had all the cards. I couldn't be beaten; I could only

throw it away. Charlotte signalled.

—Five seconds.

Time for the pleasantries.

—Good luck Rod. I think you might be in for a rough ride.

—Promises, promises.

Smart cunt, eh? No problem. He didn't even know what game we were playing.

The last ten days had been a real roller coaster. It had started with the Villa fiasco and the thing with young Tony. Seeing Jackie and Annie had been great. All Monday night, we were just pissing about together in the house. Doing family stuff.

The day after put my feet back on the ground. Dossing about, pretending to be a writer. Back to insecurity, anxiety and nightmares of a future in the building trade.

I'd been watching the lunchtime news when the phone rang. Couldn't be arsed getting it. The answering machine came on.

—Message for Paul. This is Tom Reed at Sound. Call me back or drop in at the station ASAP. We need a new presenter for Wednesday Talkback and I think you're the man for the job. It's three weeks trial for starters, but it could turn into more. I'll fill you in when I talk to you.

Hope.

I dropped in to see Tom. Didn't crack on I'd heard the message. In Tom's words: 'The cunt's only been at it for five minutes and he thinks he's Ed fucking Murrow. He demanded more money, so I demanded he fucked off out of my life.'

Tom assured me that he'd only been so blunt because he'd been thinking of offering me the show anyway. The obstruction had been cleared away.

There was no need for Tom to give me the soft soap. He'd probably been drunk when he'd fucked George off, then realised he needed someone at short notice. Either way, I didn't give a toss. This was what I'd been after for ages.

Wednesday Talkback ran from eight to ten. Classic local radio. Host, guest and the masses in two hours of lively debate. For my debut show, the guest had been some guy from Transport 2000 talking about the future of transport in London. Easy one to kick off with. Everybody's got an opinion on it. Flew by the show did.

Half the calls had come from well informed interest group bods and half from the regular mob, who phone up all the shows to say 'It's disgusting, a disgrace.' The guy from Transport 2000 was cool too. Far more entertaining than most of your activist types. I was well pleased.

Afterwards, I got a lift home off Charlotte. She lived just down the road from me, in Brixton. We stopped off at the Hobgoblin for a quick drink. Charlotte was pretty positive, but had a few criticisms. She wouldn't be capable of having an opinion until Tom told her what it was the day after. She looked a state. I suggested she went to the bog and she went all defensive. I don't know why. Her coke use wasn't exactly a secret.

Last orders. I stood up to get a round in.

—Another Becks Charlotte?

—No, I've really got to be going.

—Look. I'm sorry. I was out of order. Ave a drink. We've got to discuss next week's show anyway.

She handed me a thin folder.

—All the background on next week's guest is in there. I'll call you with some suggestions.

With that she stomped off in the way that only posh girls can. I had a drink anyway. Ended up yakking about the rapid decline of Millwall with some lads at the bar, then getting a cab home.

Jackie had waited up to tell me she'd enjoyed the show. She really meant it. Made me feel guilty for stopping off at the alehouse. Jackie went up to bed and I told her I'd only be a minute. I poured a small tot of Glenfiddich and sat down to wallow in self-satisfaction for a moment. Nothing like a job well done for perking up the soul. I picked up the file and took out the following week's brief.

Half a bottle of malt later, I drifted off into a tormented sleep, on the settee.

Jackie had the hump the morning after. I had to come the

feeble drunk. I couldn't even start to tell the truth or it would have taken us down a very rocky road. As soon as she slammed the front door, I picked up the brief. It hadn't been a bad dream. It was all there in black and white.

Name: Rod Drummond

Position: Member of the Standout Steering Committee.

Points of Interest: Stand Out is a group of radical gay men and lesbians, who campaign for equal rights and an end to discrimination against homosexuals.

Stand Out concentrate their actions against the institutions which they see as the opinion formers: the Church, the state and the media; they seek to highlight homophobic actions by these institutions in the hope that they can effect change and create a fairer, more tolerant society for all.

Personal: Rod Drummond (24) lives in Clapham and works as a legal advisor for the South London Gay and Lesbian Housing Alliance. An active member of Stand Out since his student days at Goldsmiths, he was at the forefront of last year's highly publicised rent strike against council discrimination.

Rod is spearheading the Stand Out campaign for Equal Justice, which aims to make the Police take attacks on homosexuals more seriously. Locally, Stand Out highlight the unsolved murder of Lee Turner as an example of police apathy about what they describe as: 'the ongoing holocaust against homosexual men'.

This shit wouldn't go away. It was like somebody was having a sick joke at my expense. I fought the temptation to crack open a bottle.

Briefly I thought about trying to get out of the show, but that was a non-starter. It was a busy football week so I could have blagged it, but that would have been an admission that I wasn't up to a full time contract. The only option was to go through the motions and trust myself not to blow it. I threw myself into my work. A load of bollocks statement if ever there was one. If you've got stuff on your mind it still eats away at you, however busy you are.

Saturday had been an away day to Southend with Millwall. Another sorry chapter in the Lions' fall down the table. Sunday was a far juicier prospect: Charlton v Palace. A local derby was always good for Sound, and this one had plenty of angles to exploit. Charlton were right up there in the promotion battle. A win would keep them on course for an automatic slot.

Palace needed a win too. Since relegation from the premiership the year before, all their star players had shipped out. Ron Noades had set up a continental style management structure but, basically, Ray Lewington was the first team boss. Early season, I'd really fancied them to do something. Ray bought Andy Roberts, Dougie Friedman and Gareth Taylor for decent money. Roberts and Friedman were working out, but Taylor had become a bit of a John Jensen figure.

Whenever I'd been to their games, I'd been impressed. The team were playing a pretty technical system. Back loaded, sure, but not negative.

The last few times I'd seen them, I thought the players were finally getting to grips with it. Unfortunately, time wasn't on Lewington's side. Poor results, especially at home, had seen Palace slip to just above the relegation zone. The writing was on the wall for Ray.

Us media types had built up the Charlton game as win or bust for him. It was an open secret that Harry Bassett was going to take over whatever happened. Our version made for a better story. Events and confrontation; that's what the punters want, not simmering power struggles.

Palace ground out a draw. Would that be enough to save Ray's neck?

Wednesday morning, I was down at Selhurst Park for the press conference to announce Harry's appointment. Him and Ron Noades were bullish; promotion was still possible etc. Real pro's those two. Thrived on this kind of business.

I caught a few words with Ray Lewington. The club had kept him on. Demoted him if you like. I felt for the guy. He told me he felt that things had been coming together. I agreed with him. Trouble is, in football, you need results yesterday. Ray Lewington had played a system, one he'd believed in. All it took was one know-nothing journalist saying 'why are we playing five at the back in home games?' and suddenly all the plebs are experts too. He stuck to his principles, but the results didn't come in time to save him.

Ray had a sad look in his eyes. The world can be a cruel place when you're ahead of your time.

I spent the rest of the day preparing for the show(down). Working on my game plan. Keep it general. Try to stay off the Turner case; but without being obvious. Don't be pro or anti anything. Don't come the expert. Don't say too much about anything. Think Bob Wilson.

When the red light went on I was ready. I gave Drummond a standard introduction then tossed him an open question, so that he could set his stall out.

—Homosexuals are treated as second class citizens by the ruling institutions in British society. This intolerance and persecution sets the tone for society at large. Same sex couples are denied the right to marry and face huge obstacles if they wish to buy property or adopt children. Purely because of their sexuality, lesbians and gay men have to endure a higher age of consent. These are just a few of the ways in which homosexuals suffer discrimination, but their enshrinement in law means that gays and lesbians are oppressed. This oppression is compounded and perpetuated by the media, who uphold the status quo by spewing forth hatred dressed up as fact. The result of this dual onslaught is that homosexuality is stigmatised and seen by people as wrong and in some way wicked. We are left with rampant homophobia, the only socially acceptable bigotry. Homosexuals are forced to lead secret lives; coming out means harassment at work and being ostracised from the community they live in. Those gallant enough to lead open lives are subject to scorn, gay bashing and, in the worst cases, murder. Tragically, this is exactly what happened here in South London two months ago, when Lee Turner was beaten to death in Brockwell Park. The media and the police have shown no interest in bringing his murderer to justice.

Is that it? I got a good feeling straight away. So wooden. He read all that from notes and he was still shaky. He wasn't used to this. I decided the best bet was to unleash the great British public on him.

Dave from Tooting:

—I don't agree wiv it myself, but live and let live. That's what I say. The thing is, it's alright for blokes who know what they're doing. But getting kids involved. That's sick.

Albert from New Cross:

—and after the war, I served in the Palestine Police. Now let me tell you from experience. Experience of soldiering, not the other thing. There is no way you could maintain the morale of a military unit if you had one of them in the barracks.

Jim from Catford:

—See, this isn't really our problem. I've lived in Catford

all my life and all through school and work, I never came across one. Not one. Yer see. All these so-called gay people what you get in Landan. They're all from aht in the cantry. They cam aht, or whatever it is they call it, then cam to Landan cos it's a big city. Nan of em are from rahnd ere.

Keith from Norbury:

—You guys can hide it. That's what I'm saying. You've got a choice. If you were black for just one day in this country, you'd know what oppression really means.

Maureen from Lewisham:

—I hope you'll excuse me because it's a long time since I did biology at school. But really ... the idea that a lesbian should be entitled to paternity leave seems absolutely barmy to me.

Drummond rocked back in his chair when the Nine O'clock News interrupted us. He was shell-shocked. We'd got as far from reasoned debate as was possible. I could tell he needed help, but he was too self-important to ask for it. He couldn't hack it. No gain in trying to educate bigots. Taking the piss or a plain fuck off is ten times more effective.

First up after the news was Stephen from Peckham. The bloke was definitely a plant. Probably from the same group as Rod Drummond. He was an articulate guy and the two of them started having this put up conversation, a sort of stroll round the issues Drummond had brought up in his opening monologue. Didn't even bother changing the order.

I left them to it. After ten minutes, they got on to Lee Turner. A couple of times I thought about jumping in. 'The police aren't here to defend themselves,' and all that. In the end, I went with the flow. I could have got drawn into a discussion and let on that I knew too much.

—This case is typical of the apathetic attitude of the police toward crimes with homosexual victims …

—All lives are of equal value. If the police had dedicated one percent of the resources they used on the Rachel Nickel case, to the Turner inquiry, I am sure that arrests would have been made by now …

—The police are sending out a clear message: 'We don't care if gangs of young men go out and murder queers.'

That was it. All they had. Just an idea that the coppers weren't pulling their fingers out. I nearly cheered when he said 'gangs'.

Action? A lobby of Brixton nick and a petition. Quiet, I think I hear the British criminal justice establishment crumbling to its foundations.

I felt like a weight had been lifted off my shoulders. That was the Turner thing over with hopefully and I'd not had to say a thing. With that out of the way, I could get on with being a star presenter.

Next up. Rose from Deptford:

—I can't anderstand Barrymore. E's been married to a lavly gel all these years and then e's saddenly fought—I wouldn't mind a bit of the other. Why with another feller

137

though? With is manny, e could ave any woman e wanted.

Drummond rolled his eyes and admitted defeat. He hardly said another word for the rest of the show. I had to do his job for him. Bat for the other side, so to speak. Start talking media speak, being as PC as people in public life pretend to be—i.e. ten times more than ordinary people. Then again, it's quite easy coming over all enlightened when you have guys phoning in with the burning question—AIDS sufferers: put them in camps or brand them?

—My name's Paul Andrews and you've been listening to Wednesday Talkback. The time's ten o'clock so it's over to Richard Barker with the news and sport.

Charlotte gave the clear signal.

Rod Drummond gave a little shake of the head. He knew he'd not performed. I felt like telling him not to worry, there'd be other days. I knew it wouldn't do any good. He'd been overwhelmed. I got the impression that he spent his life in meetings and workshops with people who all thought the same as him. Experts in the field. People who analysed this stuff in ivory towers.

When the hoi polloi had spoken, he didn't have an answer. He pitied them for their ignorance and bigotry. He knew he was right. Fair enough, I'd not given him much help, but it didn't matter. If he'd played a blinder the result wouldn't have been any different. The punters weren't ready to accept it yet. All round, it had been a bad day for men ahead of their time.

Charlotte gave me a lift again. This time she was gushing. She must have had some good feedback from Tom. I was due to see him the day after. It had to be about taking Talkback on full time. I'd played defensive, but the show had still been entertaining. Loud mouthed, Cockney bastards slagging off a mattress muncher made great radio.

I'd intended to go straight home to Jackie, but I ended up in the Hobgoblin again. I fancied a few pints to wind down. The build up to the show had really taken it out of me. In the end it had been a stroll. Anyway, why restrict yourself to one young woman telling you how fantastic you are, when you can have two?

A talkshow in the bag and my old sparring partner Harry appointed. That made me a Palace insider as well as a former Millwall star. And the Turner thing looked to have die on its arse. Not a bad day by any measure. Jackie was asleep when I got in. She started to stir as I squeezed her nipple. Life was sweet. I wanted to share it with her.

6th January 1994

Millwall (h)

88 to 92. Great time to be a Blades fan. Up from the Third, then straight through the Second to Division One. The Holy Grail. We followed that with two mental seasons. Not winning until Christmas, then finishing mid-table, with a club record for consecutive victories thrown in for good measure. The second year was a more standard relegation battle, but we survived. Beat the Pigs home and away too.

Great time to be a fan. For me, it was not so good. Since we'd been in the top flight, I'd been in and out of the team. The Gaffer bought Vinnie Jones early season. He looked like a direct replacement for me. Can't tell you how relieved I was when he fucked off to Chelsea. 91/92 was going fine, up till January. I was out for a couple of games with a groin strain. Unfortunately, it coincided with our annual, new year revival. The Gaffer didn't want to break up a winning team and all that crap. I only started four more games all season.

It was obvious to me that I'd have to leave. Twenty seven years old; at my peak. I needed regular first team football. Turning out in the stiffs, with the wannabes and has-beens, was doing my head in. I went to see the Boss in the close season, the week before he drew up his retain/discard list. I'd heard some rumours and I wanted to get in first. After promotion, I'd signed a three year contract for decent money. If he didn't see me as a first teamer, the odds were on Harry cashing in, while he still could. He played along and gave it, 'We'll be sorry to lose you, but if your mind's made up.' Truth was, we both knew there was nothing down for me at the Lane any more. No room for sentiment in business. Having said that, I did appreciate the disappointed act he put on.

Football was only half of it really. I wanted to get away from Sheffield. I'd fucking had it with the place. Ever since Michelle.

We'd got on sound at first; then she changed. Never wanted to go out. When she did, it was dull as fuck. Always the quiet life. Bowling, Berni Inns and all that bollocks. She had her bank head on full time:

—You need this pension.

—Join this plan.

—There's never been a better time to buy.

Thinking about the future, putting a bit away; time to settle down.

I should have seen it coming, but I didn't. He was some bloke from where she worked. Sort of a young Frank Clark without the personality. It really hit me hard. Fair enough, I'd not exactly been Old Faithful, but they were all one offs.

Deep down, I could see it was for the best. We wanted different things. For her to fuck off with an arsehole like that was taking it a bit far though. I felt a prize cunt. Kept me up a lot of nights, wondering how long they'd been at it. She said it was a recent thing, but she would, wouldn't she?

The whole Michelle business fucked me up more than I let on. I reacted in the only way I knew how. Boozers and clubs. Spouting off to the lads about how I never gave a fuck anyway, toasting my lucky escape. Shagging any old slapper. Word started getting back to the club, 'Ando's OTT on the social front.' Football's worse than the post office for gossiping old women. I told the Boss it was bollocks, but I got the feeling my card was marked.

I made up my mind one night when I was staying in. Sitting on the settee with six cans of Stella and a takeaway. There was a programme on the telly about Stan Bowles. A load of twats telling 'funny' anecdotes about the amount of cash he'd done down the bookies in the seventies. All saying the same.

—Shame it was ... we wuz at White City one night ... Ha, Ha, Ha.

I was nearly crying. Stan Bowles had more talent in his little toe than I had in my entire body, but I felt like it could be me. None of the nobodies tried to stop him. Real mates. Watch him go down the pan, then turn up in front of the cameras to have a laugh about it. It'd be the same for me as long as I stayed in Sheffield. Knocking about with a bunch of wankers, living up to my Leicester Forest image for their benefit. The star waster who the others lived off. Only difference was, I wouldn't get a Channel 4 documentary. I'd end up a minor talking point among the South Yorkshire beer monster community.

I'd only been on the list for two weeks when I got the call.

—Millwall have made an acceptable offer. Do you want to talk terms with them?

Talk terms? If they'd offered me five quid a week, I'd have took it. Millwall looked the perfect move to me. Good, solid Second Division club with ambition. I knew Mick McCarthy from my Barnsley days. Sound feller. He was blunt, as always. Said he'd heard a few dodgy things on the grapevine. I was almost straight up about it and he was satisfied. The deal went through at £250,000. That's inflation for you. Then again; it wasn't bad for a player of my calibre. After all, I did have a couple of years in the First Division under my belt. Footballwise; Millwall was everything I expected. Regular first team place. 'Pretty' football, played on the deck. In and out results. The fans took to me from the off. Everyone warms to a battler and I was performing well on a regular basis. The South London Press described me as 'a worthy heir to the mantle of Terry Hurlock'. High praise indeed.

Off the pitch, things were OK. I'd always fancied living in London. I sorted out a nice conversion flat in Forest Hill. Rented, naturally. Life in the big city was pretty quiet for me. I hardly went out at first. It wasn't some dramatic 'My Booze Hell' deal. I'd only been a social drinker, but it had got a bit out of hand. At Millwall, most of the other players lived out in Kent and Surrey, so we didn't mix socially very often. I was quite happy with the situation. I had to put my career first.

My Don Revie style dedication to being a pro lasted until Christmas 92. Because I lived nearby, I got roped into a club do at a nightclub in Lewisham. Basically, it was a meet and greet for the sponsors.

—We greatly appreciate your continued support.

—Have your photo taken with a couple of players.

—Have a drink.

—Have you thought about an ad in the programme?

The joint was full of legitimate businessmen who desperately wanted to be gangsters. I had to stand at the corner of the bar, while a succession of well to do cockneys spun me yarns about the good old days at The Den. Some old dickhead builder was sharing his memories with me, when she walked up.

—Arry Cripps. Yeah, e was ard, but e was fair. Not like nah. Nah ... Alwight Jack darling. What you been up to?

145

—Mingling.

She made mingling sound on a par with having three fillings. Lovely looking girl. Early twenties. Smart little burgundy cocktail dress.

—This is my daughter, Jacqueline. Ain't she a little darling?

She visibly cringed.

—Jack. This is Paul. Paul Andrews. He actually plays for the team. Not a bad lad either. For a northerner. Ha, ha, ha.

She nodded to me, embarrassed by her old man. I sympathised. This wasn't her natural environment. I wanted to get to know her better. Not just because she was easy on the eye either. I guessed that she'd have less Harry Cripps anecdotes than any of the others present.

—Pleased to meet you Jacqueline. Your dad's told you what I do for a living. What about you? Do you work?

I slipped into trapping mode. Step 1: Show an interest in her.

—My Jackie. She posts food parcels to our ethnic cousins.

She screwed up her face in disapproval. I raised my eyebrows.

—I work in the press office at Oxfam.

—That must be very rewarding. It must give you a great deal of satisfaction; working for an organisation that does so much good. That literally saves lives.

Naff I know, but I was a bit pissed. And it did the trick.

Her eyes lit up and she started telling me all about it. In a room full of boring pissheads, she'd found the caring/sharing guy. Her dad soon fucked off. He looked less pleased. The new Terry Hurlock had turned out to be a bit of a wet fart in his book.

Me and Jackie chatted for the rest of the night. I talked about the debt crisis and the pitfalls of government aid, with all the authority of someone who's seen Comic Relief. Her dad whisked her away before the end of the do. To him, I'd changed from Millwall hardman to smarmy cunt trying to get into his daughter's knickers. Fuck him; even if he was right. My mission had already been accomplished. I'd got her number.

I called Jackie a couple of weeks later. Took her to the dogs at Catford. My reasoning was simple. She didn't seem the type of lass who'd have been greyhound racing before. You can have a drink and a nice meal there, but it still has a slightly dodgy feel to it. A bit of rough with a sophisticated side. That was the image I was trying to put across. Catford was handy for my place, so it would give her an excuse to stay round and do the business, if everything went to plan.

That's not how it turned out. We really hit it off. Over our steak and chips, we did the standard first date stuff, but it went further. Not just, 'what do you do', and that. We're talking full life stories. Her folks were from Peckham, but they'd moved out to Southfields. Daddy sent her to private school, local not boarding, then she did an English degree at Aberdeen University. Since she finished, she'd been working for Oxfam and sharing a house in Clapham with two other birds.

Jackie kept stopping and asking if she was boring me. She wasn't. She was special. Sexy, funny, interesting, confident. We went back to mine, but we didn't fuck. We were up all night. Touching and talking. I said more to her in one night than I said to Michelle in all the time we were together. I wanted her. Not just for sex. I admired the way she could talk about herself. Her hopes and dreams, the future, the things you're taught not to mention.

She was beautiful. I wanted to be like her.

I started to see a lot of Jackie. I was well loved up. No doubt about it. Even when we had it off for the first time, it wasn't embarrassing. I was as happy as I'd ever been. Not just because of Jackie. The full deal. I realised I should have got out of Sheffield years before.

We started to go out with Jackie's mates. They were all bright young things, graduates; mainly into marketing and PR. At home, it was always the boozer if you went out. Here, it was restaurants, comedy clubs and allsorts. It's not that you can't do all that in Sheffield, it's people like me who can't. Lads. Do something out of the norm and everybody thinks you're a twat. Having a few bob means a nicer house, nicer clothes and going to posher boozers. Try going to a film with subtitles and you'll get stick off everybody for months.

Maybe it's the same in London. I never got any Millwall fans coming over to chat when I was out with Jackie's mates. They were stuck in the boozers that were officially considered 'alwight'. I didn't have to put up with that. No one was watching.

In their own way, Jackie's mates were as bad. They had their own codes to worry about: who's the most successful instead of who's the hardest; who's got the most fashionable address instead of who lives on the shittiest estate. They were a right enough bunch, but I did feel a bit of hostility from them. Jackie was one obvious reason. Charming, witty, attractive. All the blokes she knew wanted to give her one. Me turning up on the scene dashed plenty of hopes.

To Jackie's lot, people like me were letters of the alphabet in reports or a faceless mass whose best interests they discussed at meetings. They weren't used to actually meeting one of us in the flesh. Me being as smart as them got them rattled; getting the girl really rubbed their noses in it.

What did she see in me? Bit of northern rough? No. I did sometimes play the working class hero, but I didn't harp on it. Years of hanging around Jocks had shown me how dull 'it's dead rough round our way' stories can be. I had street cred. They'd have sold their mothers for it. They were all trendy and 'in the know', but I was from the other side of the tracks. I'd been around. As Jackie said; that made me 'interesting'. Perhaps I reminded her of her dad, I don't know. At the end of the day, I could fit into their world easily. Put any of those cunts in a works in Sheffield and they'd be crying for their nanny in five minutes.

Jackie got a buzz out of being a player's bird. She had a job with prospects, her old man was minted and all her mates were on the up. None of them were in the local paper every week though. None of them got stopped in the supermarket for autographs. She started coming to all the home matches. Not surprising. We soon seemed to do everything together. Unfortunately, we missed out on the play offs that season. Jackie was gutted. All she wanted was for everything to work out for me. I took it in my stride. For the first time I could remember, football wasn't the most important thing in my life.

Jackie shacked up with me in the summer. She was always banging on about Penny, one of the lasses she lived with. Usual stuff. Bringing back loads of blokes, getting stoned and listening to The Orb at full blast all night. I put it to her while we were on holiday in Turkey.

The day we got back, she loaded her car up and moved her stuff round to mine. We were sickening to be around. I even started enjoying the trips to Sainsbury's on a Sunday. I was more relaxed about life in general. When the new season came, I was playing as well as I ever had. Not just me either. The team looked real promotion prospects, early season. Something inside told me it couldn't last.

It was a chilly October afternoon. I could tell that something was up as soon as I got home from training. Jackie's car was there. I let myself in and dumped my bags in the kitchen. I'd stopped off at the deli, but I got the feeling that my lasagne wouldn't get made.

Jackie was in the bedroom. She looked like shit. Laying in the dark, pulling hard on a joint. This had to be bad. Way past work trouble. Death in the family? It couldn't be another bloke. Not this time. Not Jackie. She was too good for that. I stood at the door. She had to tell me what it was before I could do anything. Jackie sat up, stared at me, then looked down.

—I'm late.

As I went over to hug her, I could see the tears in her eyes. I held her tight and rocked her. She sobbed like a child.

—The antibiotics fucked up my pill ... Why now? ... What am I going to do? ... I've got my whole life ... my job ...

I held her for what seemed like hours. Nothing to say but the standard reassurances. Eventually I made my excuses, tucked her in and went downstairs to make a lasagne. I needed to think.

Never in the field of Italian cookery have onions been chopped so brutally. Two sensible, mature adults. How could we have let it happen? I didn't want to be like all the cunts at home. Get to their mid-twenties. Everybody else settles down and has kids then, so they've got to as well. Me and Jackie were above all that shit. We had lives to live.

Over dinner, I asked Jackie to marry me.

I carried Mrs Jacqueline Andrews over the threshold of our house in Tulse Hill on Thursday 6th January 1994.

We got married at Wimbledon registry office in the afternoon then had a meal at a hotel after. Quiet do; close friends and family only. Had to be, during the season. If more people had been there, our old man might not have shown me up so much. The cunt got worse as he got older.

Jackie looked fantastic. No matter how many times I told her, she wouldn't believe she wasn't showing.

The house was magic. Jackie's dad had put down the deposit as a present, and fixed us a good mortgage deal with 'a geezer' he knew. We had a drink, a laugh and a cuddle, then went to bed. Jackie went out like a light. She was knackered.

Up until I met Jackie, I never thought I'd want all that. Settling down like a pleb. Michelle had banged on about it morning, noon and night. If I'd given in, I'd have been fucked up good and proper. She wanted that because it had been drummed into her. Do the done thing. Same with Gary. Two kids and a divorce on his CV. That's what you get for trying to fit in.

Me and Jackie were different. The exception. We got married because it was right for us. We were in love; a concept I'd not believed in before.

As it turned out, I had to talk her into it. Promise to do my bit with the nipper and everything. I would have liked her to jack her job in for a bit, but I didn't say anything. Could've blown the lot. Even if Jackie hadn't got up the stick, I would have married her. I wanted everyone to know how we felt about each other.

She was mine. I drifted off to sleep with a smile on my face. I was planning my first kickabout in the park with Ando junior.

Crystal Palace (a)

—Another pint, Paul?

—Go on then. Why not?

Why not indeed. I deserved it. I was in a fine position. Luck? They say that about strikers, but being in the right place at the right time is more down to perseverance than good fortune.

I'd never seen so many press at Selhurst Park. I knew plenty of them from my days at the Lane. Palace v The Blades. Bassett's first game. A grudge match against his old employers. Harry wasn't actually taking over until the Monday. It was Ray's last game in charge. 0-0. Tedious as fuck. Nice sunny day for it though. Nice day all round.

Martin pushed his way back from the bar with a tray of drinks. Him and Archie had invited me to the Glaziers for a pint after the game. They were both scribblers, with the SLP and the Advertiser respectively. Weekly papers. All the rest of that mob were busy barking their copy down the phone; deadlines to meet. Archie and Martin both congratulated me at length, for getting the Talkback gig. Then it was down to business.

—Do you think Bassett will change the style of play?

—Do you think he'll bring in new faces?

—Can he work in the present structure?

I loved every minute. All the time, I was cagey. Laughing and putting on a knowing look, rather than giving straight answers. This was mainly because I didn't have a fucking clue what the answers were.

I'd played up my Bassett connections, but the only time I'd spoken to him in the last six months was at the press conference. Then he'd only agreed to give me an interview 'soon'. I knew he'd come through for me. Harry always sorted his lads out. For the moment, I was enjoying the status that being 'Harry's mate' gave me at Sound and in the bar.

Tom Reed was as quiet as I'd ever seen him. I didn't know why he'd come. He said he wanted to sort out some details about Talkback, but we'd been over that in his office, on the Thursday. Three month deal with an option for another six. Thinking about it, Tom just liked playing the journo. Getting in somewhere for free and having a drink, all that game. I'd got to know him pretty well, but I'd never heard him mention any kind of personal life, bar the odd shitty ex-wife gag. When he went out, it was always to see people about some story or feature. Family life was a distant memory to him.

That Saturday was his day off. I guess that he had nothing better to do than go to the match. Felt he needed an excuse to come for a drink. If Tom had known that I felt sorry for him, he'd have killed me.

When Archie stood up to get them in, Tom said thanks but no thanks. Me and him had to go over a few things. A problem with the show. We left. Maybe something was up after all.

On the way to his car, Tom started lecturing.

—No matter how much those cunts butter you up, don't do their job for them. Pooling information; great, we all do it. But those lazy bastards want you to write their fucking copy. It's all about having an edge Paul. People turn to us when something happens. These days scribblers are old women who can't cut it in broadcast. They want to know the score; fine. They can listen to the radio, like all the other cunts. Don't give them nothing. I had to get away from those arseholes, the crap was choking me. Let's go to the Legion.

A quick translation, from Tomspeak to English.

—There's not really any business to discuss. I want to go to another pub to get slaughtered. I'm an old newshound who's forgotten more than anyone else knows and I wasn't getting my arse kissed enough in there.

The Legion was only five minutes away, but we went in Tom's car. Tom drove everywhere.

I was less than impressed by the Legion. It was like a northern working men's club that had got lost. I half expected to bump into our old man. On the way in, I reminded Tom that I had to be somewhere later. Dinner party with one of Jackie's friends from work. I was quite looking forward to it. I'd get plenty of respect from them, because of the Talkback deal. With my sport as well, things were starting to take shape. I was still a long way off what I wanted, but I was getting there.

I wasn't just looking forward to it so I could gloat. Far from it. They were a decent bunch and the snap would definitely be top of the range. Putting a few doubters in their place would be the icing on the cake.

I went to the bar, Tom assured me we'd get off after a couple. Yeah right. I knew what his 'couples' were like. And it wasn't as if he had anything better to do. I got myself a bottle of Becks and a vodka and tonic for Tom (large one, natch).

Tom had installed himself at a table with two blokes. Good. It wouldn't look like I was ditching him when I left. When I got closer, I clocked one of them. Tom was back on form.

—Take a pew Paul. On the kiddies' drinks I see. Dave, Bob; this is Paul Andrews. He works at Sound with me. You'll have seen him before won't you Dave? He used to play for your mob.

—We've met before.

I couldn't place the face till Tom said his name. Dave: the copper from the dinner do in Wimbledon. Turned out the other guy was a DCI too. They'd been to the match; pleasure not business.

Tom was in his element. He ran the conversation, it was his show. I don't think Tom ever totally switched off from his work. You got the feeling that every question he asked was thought out; as though he was digging up background for something in the future. If Tom ever just bullshitted like a normal bloke, I got the impression he was cultivating a source. His only relaxations were talking about himself and getting shitfaced.

The copper, Dave. He was very quiet. He joined in a bit of chat we had about the match, but he said fuck all else. Just sat there, nursing a soda and lime. Another bloke who can't switch off?

A couple of times, I got the feeling that he was staring at me. When I turned round, he looked down at his drink. I didn't think anything of it. Put it down to paranoia, induced by close proximity to coppers—something we've all suffered from at one time or another.

Mostly Tom was asking about organised crime. He loved all that shit, swapping tales of notorious South London underworld figures.

A couple of VATs later, the chaps set off on a stroll down memory lane. It was time I wasn't there. Tom broke off from his anecdote about a late 70s poker game with a Turkish armed robber, to give me some shit.

—Fucking dinner party. Don't go all middle class on me Paul. I can see the thumb print on your head.

Play along. Only thing to do in those situations.

—Can't get out of it man. I'd love to stop, but our Jackie's lethal wi a rollin pin. I'll call a cab.

Dave stood up. My mate; the DCI.

—No need for that. I've got to be getting home myself. I'll give you a lift.

No shit for him. A quick round of handshakes and we were away.

There was no music in the car. Funny atmosphere. Strained. I felt like a little kid, in a car with an adult, even though Dave was only about ten years older than me. Suppose it was the size of the feller. More likely the police aspect. Eventually, we exchanged some standard football small talk, then it went quiet again. I felt very uncomfortable.

By the time the car pulled up at the end of my street, I was desperate to get out.

—Cheers Dave. Thanks a lot.

As I was unbuckling my seat belt, he turned to look at me.

—I heard your show on Wednesday night. I thought you handled it well.

—Cheers.

I got out of the car.

—I'm on the Lee Turner inquiry.

He stared at me. I wanted to shut the door, but I was frozen to the spot. He wanted to say something else, but he couldn't. We just looked at each other.

—See you Paul.

—Er ... Yeah, alright.

I shut the door and he pulled away.

Jackie was pissed off in the taxi home that night.

—What's wrong with you? I thought you were looking forward to it. Sitting there all night, not saying a word. You could tell that James and Steph were embarrassed. You ruined it for everyone.

I was too pissed to care. I made the most of the feeling. I knew there was more than a hangover in the post.

19th March 1994

Portsmouth (a)

—What's up wi yer? You've got a chance o gettin in t'Premier League. I see a performance like that first arf and I don't know what to think. You're good enough. Last week proved that. All I can think is, ya don't want it.

Big Mick was really laying in. Not surprising. If you want to have your days out at Anfield and Old Trafford, you've got to earn them in games like these. In the drizzle at Fratton Park. Forest and Palace looked good for the top two places. As long as we kept it together, I thought we were sure of the play offs. I briefly drifted off to a sunny date at Wembley in May.

—All them lads who've come down today. Spent a lot of money to get piss wet through to support Millwall. To support you. They only expect one thing in return. Effort and commitment when you pull on that shirt. Give em that and they're appy. They deserve it and I deserve it. That first alf, some of you were cheating everybody; including yourselves. We've got forty five minutes to put it right.

The second half started pretty much how the first had ended. Both teams playing tight. Neither creating anything.

0-0 would suit us both, despite the Boss's rant. Entertainment didn't get a look in late in the season. Same as Alan Durban said; if you want entertaining, go to the Palladium. Results are the name of the game.

It happened about ten minutes after half time. Geordie got caught in possession, by Pompey's winger, just inside their half. Young black lad he was. I went over to cover. No hassle. He had no support. The winger knocked it on a bit too far. It was my ball. I slid in for it on the wet turf. The lad jumped out of the way. Rode the challenge. Must've been a combination of things: my leg was at an odd angle because of the wet surface, he tried to hurdle me and keep his feet, he brushed me, my momentum fucked up his balance, he stumbled.

—AAAARRGH!

His full weight crunched my left ankle into the pitch.

The next few minutes were a blur. I was surrounded by people, but nothing they said registered. All the words merged into a distant babble. A cold, clammy feeling took over my body. I wanted to spew up. Sweat was pouring off me. I was shaking. Tears welled up in my eyes, but I managed to hold them back. A few times I thought I'd shit myself. My ring was moving out of my control. Maybe I had, maybe I hadn't.

The pain I felt when I was lifted on to the stretcher was indescribable. For the first time in my life, I knew what agony really felt like. I lifted my head up and looked down.

My foot was in the wrong place. Pointing out instead of straight forward. I fell back and stared at the grey clouds.

The St John's bods took me through into the treatment room at the back of the stand. The Pompey club doctor came in, had a shufty and told me the ambulance was on its way. There was fuck all he could do. It started to dawn on me how bad this could turn out.

The ambulance guys were reassuring. It must've been nothing to them. A walk in the park compared to scraping kids off the motorway.

—Broken leg; no worries mush.

I could see them having a cab driver chat in the canteen later on.

—You'll never guess who we had in the back today. One of them there Millwall players.

At the hospital, I was the star, new exhibit in the zoo. Gawping faces on either side as I was wheeled in. They took me straight through into a private room and put me in bed. A couple of nurses came in to wash me up and put me in a gown. Luckily, there wasn't any sludge in my shorts. Lovely young lasses; all calm and charm. They didn't know the fucking half of it. Bedside manner is cheap. It wasn't like it was their life that was in the shithouse. They left and I was alone. Totally alone for ten minutes. The doctor came and had a quick look, then it was out through the madhouse for an X ray. Back in the room, the doc told me the score in Paki-tinged medical gibberish. I picked out the word 'operation'.

Not long after, Mick came in to give me a little pep talk.

—The club'll look after you … All the lads are pulling for you … You'll be back.

Standard bollocks. I wanted him to fuck off. He was talking from the heart, but there were other vibes coming over. Pity and fear. He'd been a pro. I could feel him shouting inside.

—You poor cunt Paul. Thank fuck it never happened to me.

Not only that, I was a key player. This put a big downer on the team's prospects. On his future. He finally put us both out of our misery by fucking off.

The next hour was all loneliness. Every now and again, some of those 'wonderful' NHS bods would come in, to help prepare me. I should've phoned Jackie, but I couldn't face any more 'we'll get through this together' talk. I was relieved when they started pumping the drugs into my arm. It let me get on to the stupid operation fears that normal people have. The last thing I thought of, before I went under, was Derek Dooley.

I came round in darkness. I didn't know where I was. Agonising pain and confusion.

Never thought of the buzzer thing. Screamed my fucking lungs out until these two male nurses piled in. They gave me a shot in the arse, to calm me down. I cried my eyes out.

The second time I woke up, it was light. Everything came back to me. A nurse came in, being professionally cheery and concerned, then someone brought me a bowl of sweet mushy crap for breakfast. Some arsehole who'd been in the bed the day before had picked it.

A while later, the doc came in and told me the op had gone to plan. They'd put two platinum screws in my ankle. Too early to say how it'd turn out. I didn't bother asking the obvious question; the specky cunt didn't look like he'd understand the concept of match fitness.

Straight off, I called the Boss. He didn't crack on, but he seemed to know all the ins and outs before I said anything. He laid out the arrangements and I told him not to bother visiting me again. After an acceptable amount of pleading, he gave in.

Next up on the blower was Jackie. Predictably, she went fucking spare. Why hadn't I called before, blah, blah. I let her get it off her chest, then calmed her down by playing the wounded soldier. I apologised and offered the hectic pace of events and drugs as my defences.

She bought it. No option really.

I told her not to come and visit me. Not in her state. The club would be moving me up to a private joint near home in a couple of days. I wanted time to think. She went off on one again, and gave me the sharing speech, but I got her to promise before I hung up.

It wasn't long before I was being pushed round the hospital again. Had to have a pot put on. Right up to the top of my thigh. Bit extreme for a broken ankle I thought. Fuck it. Leave it to the professionals.

When I got back to the room, a visitor was waiting next to the bed. It was the young Pompey winger, the lad who broke my leg. He was like a cat on hot bricks. Visiting another pro, with a bad injury, is always tough. Fuck knows what it's like in that situation. He pulled the trigger, but it's me on Death Row.

I knew what he'd come for. Absolution.

—Yeah it was an accident … Don't blame yourself … All the best.

I wanted to get rid of him. Not out of any malice. Going over it wouldn't doing either of us any good. We both had to get on with our lives. Only difference was, he could walk away from it.

I spent all day thinking about my so called future. Plenty of what ifs, but no answers. I was twenty nine and married, with a kid due any minute. What if this was it? I'd been a footballer all my life. From the age of eleven, I'd been on the career ladder. Nursery team and a nod and a wink. Since then, I'd lived from contract to contract. A few setbacks, but I'd always fought back.

What if I couldn't this time? What if it's all over? I had no plans for retirement. Reckoned I had another four or five years. Plenty of time to sort something.

Not any more.

My soul searching got interrupted in the evening, when Jackie turned up. Her dad had brought her. She looked a state. Not because she was seven months gone and bloated (although that didn't help). She looked unstable. Breaking down every five minutes. I suppose it was probably to do with her being up the stick. This was why I'd not wanted her to come. She was more messed up than me about it. I was the one in the shit. I had enough on my plate, without Jackie going barmy on me. She needed reassuring.

Jackie's dad was another story. Hanging about in the background. Now and then, he'd ask me a question. The right/wrong questions; the ones I really didn't want to discuss in front of Jackie. Concerned father, or wanker putting the boot in while I was down? I never try too hard to think the best of people, because it's usually a wasted effort.

I don't know how many times I had to hug Jackie to stop her crying that day.

—Course we'll be alright. Me, you and the nipper. Everything's gonna be fine.

★

May 14th 1994: Annie Sarah Andrews born. 6 lbs 2 oz.

May 28th 1994: Millwall are knocked out of the play offs by Derby County.

'Everything's gonna be fine', eh? Actually, things did work out alright for a while. Jackie only had a month at home after the birth. She'd sorted herself out with a new job; marketing department at Courage. Miles better money and everything, but I was a bit shocked at first. She'd been so committed to Oxfam. Like Jackie said though; she could still be committed, even if she worked somewhere else. I couldn't argue with that. Barnsley, Millwall, The Blades: their fans would give anything to see the team do well. For me, they were just the cunts who paid the rent. Anyone put a few more bob in my bin, I was off. Does that make me a bad person? I don't think so.

Through the close season, I split my time between physiotherapy and being a full blown house husband. I had my second pot off in June, but I still limped a bit. The general opinion was I'd be ready to do light training around November, with a view to first team football sometime in the New Year. Made all the difference, having some light at the end of the tunnel. Something to work towards. Looking after Annie was a bind sometimes, but it was only fair I did my bit. Once in a while, I'd get pissed off. Worry about what to do, if it all went pear shaped. Planning anything would look like admitting defeat.

At times like that, I drew great comfort from the letters

sent in support by ordinary fans. Made me realise how well off I was compared to some sad cunts. The content of most of the letters was pathetic. Inspirational tales, along the lines of, 'Throughout my six months in traction, I refused to accept that I would never deliver milk again.' Misplaced sympathy. For sitting on my arse, playing with my daughter, I was drawing a lot more than they earned.

The start of the new season was a downer. First time in my adult life that I'd not been involved. I was at the game and everything; but it just felt weird. It's hard to explain. Sort of; I was there, but I wasn't part of it.

The closer I got to fitness, the better I felt. By early October, the ankle felt great. A little sore if I worked it too much, but I was definitely on the way back. Less of a leper.

It was after physio one day that I bumped into Graham from South London Sound. He took me down the boozer; said he wanted to pick my brain. Millwall were about to sign Richard Cadette and Graham made the mistake of thinking that we'd played together for the Blades. In fact, he'd been flogged to Brentford before I came back from Barnsley. Didn't matter. I was still able to fill Graham in. I'd seen enough of Cadette to know what he was about.

Graham was impressed. So much so, he asked me to work on the Millwall/Blades game with him, on the 29th. I enjoyed it to the full. I'd always thought about getting into that kind of thing, but I was waiting for someone to ask me. You know how it is.

I was as good as I thought I'd be. I couldn't say exactly what I wanted. After all, Millwall paid my wages and the lads were my workmates.

MILLWALL 1 SHEFFIELD UNITED 0

Shit game. Should've been 0-0. Cadette saved the day. Injury time winner, on his home debut, against the mob who dumped him. Fairy tale stuff.

Graham asked me how I was fixed for doing the odd stint on the mike with him. I really fancied it, but I was back in training the week after. I had to devote every effort to my comeback.

Nov 7th 1994: Back in for light training.

Nov 28th 1994: Huge improvement in mobility. Start full training with the lads.

Dec 1st 1994: First full scale practice match. I stumble unchallenged and crumple to the turf. I am rushed to hospital.

Dec 20th 1994: The specialist tells me that this break will restrict my ability to move my foot. It is his professional opinion that I will never play competitive football again. Wayne's World on TV.

Jan 20th 1995: After listening to a number of medical opinions, Millwall Football Club contact me officially. They inform me of their intentions. They are to terminate my contract and cash in the insurance.

Feb 27th 1995: The club and the PFA official acting on my behalf negotiate the termination of my contract. The matter is settled amicably. At the age of 30 years and 115 days, Paul Andrews retires from football.

Millwall (a)

I'd been up all night, on and off. Tossing and turning. It wasn't just insomnia either.

Panic attacks. Shooting pains in my chest. Knowing it was all in my mind didn't help either. Every time, I thought: 'This is it.' Never was though.

Everything had been hunky dory. The garden had rarely looked fucking lovelier. Then the Palace match had come round. That fucking rozzer. He knew something. My mate Davie. Detective Chief Inspector Knowles. That bloke never did anything without a purpose. His little comment. The timing; everything. No way was this paranoia. I'd got over that a while back. Deliberate was that cunt's middle name. For a start, he knew where I lived. At the Legion, I'd told him Tulse Hill. That and only that. He dropped me right on the end of my street. He was letting me know he'd checked me out. Only explanation.

Inspector Knowles knew fucking plenty. No doubt. The question was; exactly how much and what was he going to do about it? Did he have evidence? A witness or some forensics? Surely not. It'd be official then. They wouldn't let him piss about playing at Columbo. No such thing as maverick coppers in real life. It wouldn't be up to him anyhow.

He probably just had some hunch. When I'd got out of the car, he'd mentioned the Drummond show. Had he spotted something? I'd gone over it a million times in my head, but I couldn't remember letting anything slip.

Was he playing me or warning me? If he suspected me, he might be trying to push me into action. Slipping up. Giving him something concrete to build a case on. Or he might be tipping me the wink: they're on to you Paul lad, get the fuck away while you still can.

There was a third option, one that I would have loved to be true: I was imagining it all. Mr Knowles, the friendly detective, had merely thrown away some platitude about the show and I'd fantasised the rest. A fair enough assumption, but if you'd been there, seen the way he said it, you'd know it was shit.

That look. There was something behind it. He nearly spilled it too. Whatever he was holding back, I had to know. Today was the day.

I shagged Jackie before I got up. Doggy. It was the only practical way, given the size of her. She still had a couple of months to go and she was already more bloated than she'd ever been with Annie. We'd been having it off a lot. I'd developed a sort of pancake day mentality towards sex. I could be going away at any time, so I had to have my fill, just in case. It kept Jackie happy too. Reassured.

I passed on Jackie's offer of breakfast. I needed to bust the fuck up out of there and get on with it.

I caught a 68 bus on Norwood Road. The only way to travel. I got off halfway to the ground, at Camberwell Green, and ducked in MacDonald's for a 'big' breakfast, to break the journey. I was miles too early and busting for a shit. Time for the age old debate. Stick or go. The bogs were always clean enough, but you got the staff eyeballing you big time. Every crapper was a potential junkie to them. I decided against. Once you start with that game, you can't stop. Invariably a letdown too. Waiting for an almighty plop and getting a feeble spit. The lock would probably be fucked anyway. I'd hang on. One good thing about the 'New' Den. Pristine toilets. Not like the old days. I remember being a young un, at the Lane. You could tell how big the crowd was, by how far above your shoes the piss was. Not any more. Say what you like about Millwall's ground: no atmosphere, no home advantage like the old place, but the shithouses are spotless. At the end of the day, that's what matters to the punters. Isn't it? Somebody has lost the plot somewhere along the way.

I was on edge. It was my gig and I didn't know what was happening. Five weeks since the Palace game. Enough stewing time for anyone. Today's match provided the perfect cover: Millwall versus The Blades. I'd set it up a fortnight before.

—Alright Dave. It's Paul ... Paul Andrews ... Jackie works for brewery ... complimentary executive tickets ... and I thought, who do I know in London, who's a Blade?

Course he took the bait. Free beer, meal and box ticket. Who wouldn't? Top day out by anybody's standards. How could I be sure what was going on? Perhaps this was what he wanted. By making a move I'd confirmed his suspicions. He could reel me in. Whatever. Time to find out. I had no plan. Play it by ear. No choice.

12:30. Dave turned up at the player's entrance. Bang on time; to the fucking second. Totally in character. Tom had told me that he was dead straight. Whatever the opposite of a maverick is. Punctuality is second to nothing for cunts like him. I gave my 'mate' the full behind the scenes guided tour. All your punters love that. I mean, one dressing room is the same as the next, but people buzz off the insider vibe. DCI Knowles was suitably chuffed. Put him at ease. Soften him up. Lull him. I was on home territory.

We ended up in the exec suite, round the back of the East Stand. Had a couple of drinks. He knew a few people there. South London copper. Bound to, wasn't he? After about an hour of socialising, it was time to go our separate ways. I had work to do and Dave had a meal with a bunch of suits to endure. I arranged to meet him after the game. He seemed to be having a whale of a time.

I couldn't get my head round it. He didn't have a care in the world. I'd been watching him all day and he just seemed to be having a good time. A bit uptight, but that was normal for Dave, as far I could see. It didn't matter. The cunt was holding something back. I'm never that wrong.

MILLWALL 1 SHEFFIELD UNITED 0

Shit game. Should've been 0-0. The Blades were still in the mire. They didn't lose much, but they won even less. Millwall; where do you start? The slide had started before McCarthy went. The club's choice of replacement surprised me. Jimmy Nichol. Done wonders with Raith; trophies, Europe and all that, but it's a different ball game south of the border. I mean; how many managers have been a success in Scotland then done the business in England? OK: Alex Ferguson, fair enough, but try naming another one. See what I mean. The three points made the lads look safe, for another year at least.

Fuchs got the winner. Should put a few quid on his price tag, when he finally gets his move. When the time came, I wondered if anyone would have the bottle to use it? That once in a lifetime headline:

'UWE FUCHS OFF.'

I did the post match stuff on auto pilot. The interviews always seem pointless to me. Everyone tunes in to keep up with the score and to get the other results. After the report, all that's left is a load of hanging around for some tosser to come out and trot out whichever batch of clichés fits the bill. You didn't have to be Mystic Meg to predict what was coming that day.

—We've played better and lost ... I hope we have turned the corner ... Difficult games coming up ... Games against Palace are always tough, the one in a fortnight will be even more so ... The run in's tricky, but there aren't any easy games in this league ... With the quality and spirit we've got here, we'll definitely stay up ... Cheers Paul.

On the way to the Exec, I couldn't help wondering if I used to give interviews like that. Suppose I must have. What's the fucking game, eh?

I was ready for a few pints, but I had to stay on the ball. See where the Davey boy thing was going. When I got to the bar, Dave Knowles seemed far from threatening. In fact, he came over as chilled out as I'd ever seen him in the time I'd known him. And was he fucking grateful. He thanked me so much I nearly started blushing. I relaxed as well. I felt relieved and daft at the same time. I had been that wrong. There was nothing going on, except in my head. To put it mildly, I'd over reacted.

A couple of pints later, everyone started to drift off. The suite would be shutting in a while. It was make your mind up time: call it a day or make a session of it? Easy call. I'd been hyped up for weeks. Over nothing by the looks of it. A blow-out was just what the doctor ordered. My new pal was well up for it. Dream day out for him; I felt like Jimmy Saville on a trip to Disney World with a dying mong. Fuck, I deserved a bit of thanks after what the cunt had put me through.

The evening's festivities kicked off in the Canterbury. A Millwall geezers' pub. Every fucker in there recognised me, but none of them acknowledged it. They all went out of their way not to let on, show they were too hard for that caper. Paul Andrews: nothing special. Not bowing down to that cunt. Suited me fine. I just wanted a quiet pint or eight; not an episode of All Our Yesterdays with some cockney tosspots. We had a couple, then got a minicab to Camberwell. I'd had enough of the Old Kent Road for one night. Doing the crawl down there, just to show I could, would have been a waste of effort. Dave knew the score.

We settled down for a sesh in the Hermit's Cave. Tidy little boozer. Straddles the tightrope between New, 'something in the City' Camberwell and Old, 'wanna buy a video' Camberwell. Man, we put some ale away. He turned out to be alright Dave, for a copper.

All the conversation was as you'd expect from a pair of old-time Blades. Being a lad around Sheffield, great games, the changing face of town pubs. We both laughed a lot. Dave was over excited about everything. I got the impression that he didn't get pissed much. Didn't hang loose very often. I suppose he found it easier, as he was with one of his own.

I enjoyed myself too. Everything had been getting to me, but here I was. Back in business. Sitting across the table from DCI Knowles of Brixton nick. The man whose professional life was currently dedicated to arresting the killer(s) of Lee Turner, and he hadn't got a fucking clue. I remember it dawning on me. I must have got away with it. The last two weeks had shown that it'd always plague me but, as far as the law was concerned, it must be over.

A couple of times, I nearly asked him about it. I did have an excuse after all. I'd done a show about it and he'd brought it up the other time. I could put my mind at rest, once and for all. I fought the urge. Wrong time. If there's ever a right time and place to ask about stuff that might lead to life imprisonment, a boozer when you're pissed up to your eyeballs isn't it.

Leave it be Paul lad. It's all over. Stop torturing yourself and smell the flowers.

The bell went. Dave got them in; then he pitched me. Invited me back to his for the Bruno fight. Everybody had been on about it all day. I'd got Sky at home, but I'd not got my arse in gear to buy the package. I didn't take much persuading. Dave was well keen. He seemed eager to pay me back for the day out. Promised me as much grog and takeaway as I could handle. Sold.

I didn't fancy going home to Jackie in a tacking. She'd be all tired and emotional. Best for all concerned if I stayed out. Dave didn't have any trouble and strife at home. He'd used that as a selling point for piling round his for the fight. Then he seemed apologetic. Bit sad. The grass is always greener I suppose. Poor cunt. Least I could do was go round to keep him company and empty his fridge.

12th August 1995

Barnsley (h)

First day of the season. Crystal Palace v Barnsley. One of my old clubs against, near enough, my local club. Lovely sunny weather. I had every reason to look happy. I bumped into Martin from the South London Press. The smile and the handshake seemed genuine enough.

—Alwight Paul. What brings you down ere?

—I'm doin the match, for Sound.

—Yeah. Ow's that going then?

—Alright. Ya know.

—Who you working with; Bob?

—Bob's left. I'm commentating. We're carryin it live, seein as there's no Premier League on.

Freeze it right there.

The look on his face. Respect. Bit of envy? Surprise that a washed up old peg leg was good for anything but grunting the odd comment to a 'real' broadcaster. Whatever else, he was impressed. It was great to see that look again.

For a while after retiring, it had been pretty rough. The old cliché is that your fair-weather friends fuck off and you find out who your real friends are. Not true. You find out that there's no such thing as real friends. People want to knock about with you because of who you are. If you're not that any more, why should they want to knock about with you? Family: yes. Friends: no way. No commitment. It hurts until you learn to deal with it. Till you suss out that they're all bastards. All I had was Jackie and Annie.

Boredom and self pity. I did fuck all for a couple of months. Never used to leave the house; except for physio. I loved Annie to death, but the constant screaming and shitting would test anybody. To me it was another brick in the wall. The depression weighed a ton. It's a vicious circle. Don't want to go out. See cunts either looking smug or feeling sorry or both. So stay in. See nobody. Do nothing. Nothing happens. No opportunities. No way out.

I cried a couple of times. I'd not done that for years. Every time, it was over stupid stuff that I didn't give a fuck about. The boiler going on the blink and some documentary about some blind kid. The boiler was the worst. Domestic hassle. I should've been out at work ... somewhere, not dealing with menial, household shit. Having to take Good Old Mr Plumber giving me the Blue Peter guide on: 'How To Not Fuck Up Your Central Heating'. When he fucked off, I started sobbing. Thirty years old and useful to fucking no one. If there'd been a gun in the house, I might have used it, the way I felt.

I resented Jackie. I relied on her totally. That terrified me. She was a roaring success in her new job. Marketing/PR: As far as I could see, it was one long fucking piss up full of beautiful people hatching plots to rip off the plebs. Very fucking smart. All that time on my own to think. It was unhealthy. How long was Jackie going to put up with it? Work was a non-stop, social whirl; then she had to come home to a fucked up cabbage. She must get offers. Being in a scene like that must turn your head. Plant a few ideas. Even if her work mates didn't, her old man would have a go at splitting us up. No fucking doubt about that. My head was chocka with shit like that. The rows got worse.

It all came to a head. I kicked off on Jackie. I'd cooked her a chicken dinner and, when she came in, she'd already eaten. Sad or what. Anyway, it all came out and I mean all. As us commentators say, 'No quarter asked and no quarter given.' Horrible it was. Neither of us stormed off. We just took it in turns; making the other feel like shit, until we were as low as it was possible to get. Then we sat in silence; looking at the wreck opposite.

—If you could do anything; what would you do?

I thanked God that Jackie spoke first. Soft, concerned, caring; her eyes begging me to let her in. We talked like we used to before the injury. Before Annie. About the future. Hopes. I told her I wanted to try and make a career in the media. I blurted it out. It was the first time I'd told anybody, even though I'd thought about it for years.

I felt embarrassed. That night, I remembered why I fell in love with Jackie. She took me seriously. She believed in me. Support and inspiration. We're in this together. She was gorgeous.

When Jackie's on the case, things happen. She brought home loads of stuff about courses that her luvvie friends had recommended. Radio Journalism and Presenting. She gave me confidence. I ended up doing a six week crash course at some BBC place in Clerkenwell. Didn't come fucking cheap either. I felt a bit of a dick, in with all the other starry-eyed cunts, but it's the price you pay. At the same time, I was looking for work. I did a few bits for South London Sound, mainly riding shotgun on commentary games. They had nothing more going, but at least they didn't give me a straight fuck off. The radio game's like football. To get a contract, you've got to plug away. Take any chance you get. Prove to the Boss that he needs you.

Jackie kept me up. Kept encouraging me to try things. Pushing me. Kicking me up the arse. I had some direction. A month before the beginning of the season, I got a call from some guy at Sound. Asked me to do a few dummy commentaries on friendlies. Said they needed a back up, just in case anything happened to a regular. I did two pre-season matches at Dulwich Hamlet into a tape for them. Later that week, I got a call from Tom Reed. A member of the sports team had left, 'by mutual consent'. Could I step in? Match to match. Strictly casual. See how it goes.

Light.

Blood and guts. End to end. Top quality fare. I had a quick one after, then went home. Jackie had done me a hotpot. The phone rang at about eight o'clock. Tom Reed; telling me I'd done a good job. That night was sound. A few glasses of wine with Jackie. May not sound like much, but it was. I felt like I was on the up. Dreaming again. I had a lot to learn, but I was sure I could make it.

All I needed was a break.

17th March 1996

WBC Heavyweight Championship of the World
'Iron' Mike Tyson v Frank Bruno
(CHALLENGER)   (CHAMPION)

Comes to Anderson ... Still Anderson ... Is he going to have a go ... YEEAASS ... A superb finish by Anderson ... Gave the keeper no chance.

—Remember that one do ya Paul?

I looked up slowly. The combination of ale, a bellyful of pizza and a comfy chair had almost put me to sleep. 'Sheffield United's 100 Greatest Goals', or something like that, was on the telly. The kind of video that's only ever watched by pissed up blokes, waiting for the boxing from Vegas. The idea of watching it alone or sober would be sick; nay obscene.

Peter Anderson's goal against Sunderland was on. The one that won Goal of the Month.

—Aye.

—Won Goal o t'Month.

—Aye.

—That'll ave bin about 78 won't it?

—Aye.

—Or were it before?

191

—No. 78.

It was definitely 78, because Sabella was playing and Happy Harry Haslam signed him straight after the World Cup. One season and it was down to the Third. I was too pissed to offer a full explanation to Dave, but he bowed to my superior knowledge anyway.

—Were ya there?

—Aye.

I realised I wasn't saying much. Better have a stab at conversation.

—I were about 13. There were ell on after. They'd just started building that dual carriageway between Shoreham Street an Bramall Lane. Rocks an concrete flyin allo'er t'place.

I stopped myself. It didn't seem right talking about that kind of thing in front of a copper. Even though it was only kid's stuff, from yonks back. It went quiet for a minute. I'm sure Dave looked a bit envious. He'd never been a lad. I'd only played at it when I was a kid, but he'd not even done that. No coppers have. You can tell. All the ones I knew were goody-goody, soft gits when they were at school. Scared of everything. They pretend, same as footballers I suppose, but they can never go the full distance. If they did, they'd not get a job in the first place. Thing with coppers though, is they all come over as wannabe lads. Can't get it out of their systems. Wanting to be street-smart hardmen. Maybe that's why they spend their lives hiding behind a uniform, dishing out shit to the genuine article. Envy.

—Ready for another?

Dave stood up and pointed at his empty glass. I nodded agreement.

—Aye. Cheers.

Good old Dave. OK, so he was a copper and a bit of a boring twat, but he was a fine host. I only wish he'd offered coffee. I was totally bloated. Last thing I needed was more beer.

Dave disappeared off to the kitchen. Not a bad wee gaff he had. Two bed conversion flat at Streatham Hill. Pretty much like the one I'd had in Forest Hill, except it had a garden and was a lot tidier. Very bare though. Take away the telly and the video and you wouldn't know anybody lived there. Must be a story behind why a DCI lived in a place like that, but I was fucked if I wanted to hear it.

I felt something scratching at my leg. Dave's dog. One of those pointless, little hairy ones. I gave it a kick and told it to fuck off. It started yapping and going berserk. All I fucking needed. The row the mutt made brought home to me how pissed I was. It was getting on for three, but the fight was still a couple of hours off. I would have been much happier crashed out at home. The night had fizzled out, but nobody was prepared to admit it. Then again, who knows? By police standards, it was probably a hoot, this watching vids malarkey.

Dave came back with more beers. Those ones in little

bottles that everybody has. I thought: aye, aye; even the coppers have got somebody on the Calais run. Then he made a point of explaining how cheap they were at Sainsbury's. Tosser.

Easy there Paul lad. Don't go upsetting everybody.

He sat down and the excuse for a dog went over to him.

—As e bin botherin ya?

I lyingly shook my head. Dave picked up the hairball and started stroking it.

—All I've got left, aren't ya Arry?

I could see where this was going and I didn't like it one bit. He looked over to me, then nodded at a small picture on the side. A woman and two kids.

—Left two year back.

He was past the point of no return. Here we fucking go.

—You're a married man aren't ya Paul?

—Aye.

—Kids?

—Aye.

He wanted more.

—Annie's nearly two an there's another on t'way.

—Are ya appy?

For fuck's sake. I just stared back at him. I didn't want any part of this.

—Sorry. (Big sigh) I used to think we were.

Inside my head, I was shouting. Shut the fuck up man. Get a grip of yourself. It was too late. He plodded on. The long hours. Dedication and providing. The shock of finding her with another man. A copper. A colleague. Two and a half years they'd been at it. Laughing at him. He would've taken her back, even after all that, but she didn't want to know. They were last heard of running a B&B in Aberystwyth. Sounded like Nirvana, the way he said it. Poor bastard.

I wanted away badly. Once a drunk starts on his sob story, that's it. I went for a piss. In the bog, I did the full Vincent Vega bit. I'd give it five minutes, then I'd make my excuses. I went back to the front room and sat down. I wanted to say something. A bit of small talk to get him off the subject. My mind was blank. Dave's wasn't.

—If she'd not left … It would never've started.

He said it deliberately. As though he'd practised it. Dave stared at me. He looked nervous. Breathing heavy. I knew I was supposed to say something, but I didn't have the energy. I reckoned if I let him ramble on, he might drop off, then I could do the offmans.

—I've never told anybody this. You understand Paul. You're one of the lads … from ome. You know what the score is.

Just my fucking luck. An accident of birth means I cop for this cunt whining.

—I've almost phoned ya loads o times, but I cun't. When ya got in touch about t'match … I knew I ad to today. I've bin avoidin it. Ya know … We've ad a few beers an a laugh

195

... Good day out ... It never seemed t'right time.

He was a state.

—I've got to get it off my chest ... Tell someone. Someone who'll understand.

It was like a bad episode of Ricki Lake. Spit it out man. You've got problems—you should've been over to my house lately. So his wife had fucked off. Sure I felt for him, but wallowing in misery and over dramatising his problems wasn't doing either of us any good.

—It's bin turnin me inside out. Especially t'last few months. Since I've been on t'Lee Turner case.

Whack. I felt like a cartoon character who'd copped for an anvil. He'd said the magic words. The anxiety shot through my body, flushing out the drunken apathy. Screaming sobriety took its place. Surely the cunt hadn't been fucking with me all along? I had to get back on the game plan. Stay calm. Let him make the running. Don't give anything away. Dave was getting himself together. I tried to look sympathetic.

—After Mary left, I ad nothing. I were a shell. The boys, the ouse, everythin. Gone. People say start again, but I couldn't see the point. You've got no idea ow it urt. I ad less than nothin.

He stared at me. Seemed like he was letting some anger pass.

—Must be knockin on for eighteen month ago ... Since it started.

Dave took another deep breath. He was looking everywhere, apart from at me. He started to roll, fitfully.

—I'd taken Arry down to Streatham Common. Late on it were. Bout one in t'mornin or summat. I'd not got used to gettin to sleep wi'out Mary there. Never ave ... Even now.

He gave a sad little smile. I raised an eyebrow as I nodded. I needed him to go on, not get bogged down in slush. It was time to sort shit out. Find out what he was holding. Dave took his prompt.

—Anyroad. The Common were as quiet as it ever is. I ad a bit of a lark round wi Arry for about twenty minutes, then eaded back up to t'car park. There'd bin a bloke, bout your age. Early thirties. E'd bin anging about when we got there. When I got up to t'car park, e were still there. Like e were waitin. E got in is car, one o them little Fiat Pintos, and just sat there. I were looking o'er at im, wonderin what e were up to. Well, not exactly. Ya know. I am a copper. I know the kinda thing that goes on down t'Common.

He paused. Seemed embarrassed. Made a point of showing he was street-smart. Pride always drops you in it. Dave took a swig of his beer. This wasn't anything I'd expected. Up to press, it didn't have any bad implications for me. I still had to hear the lot to make sure.

—I got in t'car, an I can see in t'mirror, e's still lookin at me. E put is lights on, an sat there for a bit longer, then e drove up right next to me. I looked over, an e were starin straight at me, an e ad is dick in is and.

Dave delivered the last bit with some (mock?) shock. Bit late for the bluster I thought, but I played along. It was clear that the copper was going into a tricky section.

—E pulled off an stopped, at t'entrance. E looked round an cocked is ead; like I should follow im. I don't know why, but I did.

More beer and head shaking. Looking at me with appealing eyes.

—E went over t'ill, then left, towards Gypsy Ill. The opposite way from ere. I cunt even kid mysen that I weren't following im. E pulled up on a road near t'TV mast, an went in an ouse. I dint know what were goin on. How to act or owt. E stood at t'window; starin at me. Must've bin about ten minute. Arf the time, I cunt stand to look. Eventually, e came to t'door an waved for me to come in. An ... I went in.

Dave looked up. He had a simple expression. Like a mug who's just done his wad in the bookies. Gutted but strangely content.

If he thought that was the end of the story; he had another think coming. Alcohol sometimes gives you a real sense of focus. No way was he getting off the hook. I needed to know the details and what it had got to do with me.

—What appened?

That shook him.

—When?

I glared at him. He'd dragged me into this. He realised it was too late to back out at this stage.

—You know. We like touched each other ... Hugged ... An then ... we wanked each other off.

It took a lot of getting there, but it seemed to relax him. I nodded again. Let him know I wasn't judging him. He loosened up.

—Like I say. That were t'first time. I'd not looked at a woman since Mary. An blokes ... never. After that appened ... I don't know. At t'time, it were fine, but for weeks after, I felt terrible. Ashamed ... Ashamed and confused. I were sure it were a one off ... But I were lonely ... An it appened again an again. Streatham, Brockwell, Clapham, Ampstead, even t'South Coast. Every time, I swore it'd be t'last, but I knew I wunt be able to elp mysen t'next time. When I think of t'risks I took ... You know ... I'm a copper ... A DCI for God's sake. How do you think it would've gone down if I'd bin caught?

I felt for the guy. I knew what he was going through, more than he did. More than he'd ever realise. Or was it? Why had he singled me out?

—Then the Turner case ...

Trying to look calm was getting unbearable. My heart was beating out of its cage. Sweat in the eyes, the grip on my bottle close to breaking point. Revelation time. I was at a point where I had no clue what he was going to say. The cruising shit had already thrown me. Did he have any shit on me or not? I just needed it to be over.

—I were too close. I knew too much. That lad Drummond, the one you ad on yer show. Im and is mob know. They saw through it. No one else. No one else gives a damn. Especially not the force. Dead puffs aren't a very igh priority.

—What are ya sayin Dave? What's the crack? You've bin oldin summat back? There's some kinda cover up? What?

He looked at me like I was an idiot. Like he'd spelled it all out and I was too thick to grasp it. I was scared.

—Course I am. Can't ya see? I were there. I were in t'park wi Arry. I saw Turner t'night e died. I know everythin.

I was paralysed. In my head, I could hear keys turning and mad screaming. Nobody knew I was here. Attack? Run? Deal? Offer? Touch? Sit tight. Hear the lot. See what he's got. The cunt was disintegrating in front of me.

—When I got the call, it knocked me out. I were stunned. I cunt say I'd sin im. It could've led to ... ya know. It could've come out. After that, it were too late. For months now ... It's bin ell. Lads on t'case. All t'jokes an that, bout people like me. The psychologists' reports on t'kind o people who cruise parks. Sad lonely losers. Can't come to terms wi t'way they are. Low life. Every day, I've to listen to em talk about me. Don't ya see? It may as well've bin me. It nearly were me. I passed Turner. I thought about it. I ated is type. Young an andsome. The way they were, wi

200

blokes like me. Arrogant. Laughin and sneerin at us desperate old closet queens … cos that's what I am, int it? I used to urt em. I'd lose it. I hated mysen for bein there, so I'd tek it out on them. It were just rough, but sometimes … it got a bit out of and.

Dave lit a ciggie.

—It could've bin me; killin or bein killed. If it goes on, it might be me next time. It's a bloody mess. I dint want this; any of it. You understand, Paul. You've got to. I can't elp it. I ad to tell someone.

The bloke was in bits. I'd managed to keep up my front. Dave was practically eating his fag. He was openly begging and threatening. As far as I could make out, he had fuck all on me. What was I supposed to do? Tell him everything was going to be alright? Hug him? Any words of comfort might backfire later.

The atmosphere was too charged to play cool. I'd got what I wanted. Sitting around had no plus points.

I stood up and walked to the door. I didn't even look at him. This wasn't my problem any more.

Post Fight Analysis

I woke up at eleven. To be more accurate, I woke up for the second time at eleven.

A couple of hours earlier, Jackie had been stomping around the room, chuntering about something. She came in and announced that we were going to her folks' for the day. Barbecue and all that carry on. Been arranged for ages, apparently. We had a frank discussion about the matter, then she called me a pissed up bastard and fucked off in the car with Annie.

At the time, I thought she was a bit OTT. There was always a kick off about going there. All that happy families bollocks; Jackie knew how much I hated it. I married her, not them. Never usually got that heated though. I found out what the underlying problem was when I rolled into it. A big, soaking wet patch of piss. Must have done it during the night. The moment of self-disgust passed. It had been my first heavy session on the beer for a while. After a bit, you learn to live with these little mishaps. I wasn't sure Jackie ever would though.

As it went, I was quite glad she'd cleared out for the day.

I fancied a lazy Sunday dossing round the house on my own. I ran a bath and put the radio on. A soak and a ponder.

The news from across the Atlantic was bad. Old Frank Bruno, eh? I'd really thought he stood a chance as well. Tyson was the better fighter, no question about that, but all that time inside, away from the game—I thought that would've taken the edge off him. At the end of the day, it sounded like Frank didn't believe in himself enough. When it came to the crunch, he couldn't hack it. No amount of training's going to change that. That was the end of Bruno as a boxer, surely.

Obviously, I didn't really give a shit about Big Frank's career prospects. It was just easier to make sense of the night before in Las Vegas, than it was to make sense of the night before in Streatham.

I'd walked home from Dave's, then crashed out. I never blacked out totally when I was drunk, but sometimes it took a while for it to come back; bit by bit. Even more so that day. It'd all been so unreal. In the cold light of day, I came to the same conclusions as I had the night before. I was in the clear. The weeks of fretting had been for nothing. I'd never been under suspicion and the trail was so cold, the odds were lengthening that I ever would be.

But it hadn't been entirely paranoia. The copper had been trying to tell me something alright. It fucked me up for a bit, sussing out why he chose me. Made sense in a way.

That shit was doing him in. He needed to open up. Who else was he going to tell? The blokes at work?

—By the way lads. That murder case we've bin on for t'last few month. I've bin withholding evidence, cos it might expose my double life as a shitstabber.

Yeah, I'm sure the boys at Brixton nick would've been very supportive. His mates, then? The Sporting Club chaps. Very sensitive to the traumas of coming out no doubt.

I suppose he saw me as being like him. Same background. Left home to get on in a geezerish career. Thing was, he'd heard the talkshow that night, so he knew I had a caring side; that I'd risen above all that macho bollocks. Sheffield lad about town turned woolly liberal. I must have looked tailor made. Dave needed someone to understand him. Absolution for his sins from Paul Andrews: football hardman. Mr Northern Bloke Culture himself. I would've loved to, but it wasn't on. He didn't know the score. Say the wrong thing and it might have set the blue lights flashing in his head. Then he could whip out the handcuffs, crack the case and put it all behind him.

I got out of the bath and towelled off.

I reckoned I'd got everything as straight as it was going to be. I threw on a tracksuit. It was going to be one of those days. When I went downstairs, I noticed the red light flashing on the answering machine. I hit the button and Dave Knowles' voice croaked out of the speaker.

—Paul ... Are ya there? I called to say sorry. I'd no right

to drag you in. It's a fuckin mess … but it's my mess. It's up to me to sort it out. Gettin it off my chest elped me mek up my mind. There's not goin to be any more lads in parks. I'll see to that. Thanks for listening … for bein a mate.

He sounded like shit. I did 1471. He'd called at 5:20. Me and Jackie must've been spark out. 'Thanks for bein a mate'—some fucking mate I am Dave lad; fucking off when you needed me. I listened to it again. When he said 'fuckin', I cringed. I'd never heard him swear before. Then again, I hardly know him. And I'm his best mate. Doesn't say much for the bloke really.

I nipped around to the shop for the papers and something microwavable, then sprawled out on the front room floor. Time to catch up on the week's events.

Half an hour into my vegging session, the doorbell went. I opened the door. Two plainclothes coppers. I was desperately hoping I didn't look as shocked as I felt.

—Paul Andrews? I'm Detective Sergeant Milnes from Brixton and this is Detective Constable Sanderson. Can we have a word?

—Yeah … er … come in.

My head was chocka. Double bluff? Parallel investigation? Witness? 'Lucky' break? We went through to the front room. I started clearing the papers up. I stopped myself. Stop being jumpy. Then again, how are you meant to act when two sids drop round on a Sunday avo? The coppers both sat down. Got to be a good sign. The DS set the ball rolling.

—Do you know Dave Knowles?

—Er ... Yeah. I met him a few month back. Sin im around a few times since. An we went to t'match yesterday. Millwall/Sheff United.

—Dave Knowles died this morning.

No need to act. I was speechless. Stay calm. Play it by ear. Shit. I was so used to being guilty it trumped the fact that I hadn't done this one. I was cabbaged.

—How?

—Looks like suicide. A gunshot was reported by a neighbour at 5:40 this morning. The officers who attended found him slumped in a chair, with a fatal gunshot wound to the head. There was a Berretta pistol on the floor, next to the body. It was registered to DCI Knowles. Like I say; it looks like suicide, but we have to investigate any suspicious deaths.

I felt some relief. The coppers were just going through the motions. Doing their job. There were a million and one ways they could have known I'd been with Dave the day before. No cause for alarm. They didn't mean me any grief.

—What we want to do is put together a picture of Dave Knowles' final hours. What he was doing, his mental state and all that kind of thing. So could you talk us through the time you spent with DCI Knowles yesterday?

I got the distinct impression that Dave wasn't going to be greatly missed by his brother officers. Rivalry? Personal? Aloofness? Who cares?

—I met im at t'ground, bout arf twelve. We ad a drink, then I ad to work. I were commentatin for South London Sound. Afterwards, we ad a drink in t'executive lounge, then went for one on t'Old Kent Road. Then, we got a cab to t'Ermit's at Camberwell. At closin, we got a cab back to is, to watch the fight. We ad a few bottles and a pizza, then I got off. Come back ere.

—What time was that?

—Dunno. Bout three.

—How did you get home?

—Walked it.

The other, younger, copper piped up.

—Why did you leave then? You said you'd gone round for the fight. That didn't come on till nearly five.

—I'd ad enough, ya know. I were ammered. I just wanted my bed.

Young Sherlock seemed to buy it. It was more or less the truth anyway. The fatter, more chilled out copper took up the running again.

—How did he seem when you left him? What was his state of mind?

—Er … E were the worse for wear; ya know. We'd ad a session.

—What kind of a drunk was he? Happy drunk?

Miserable drunk?

—Ard to say. Just drunk. Bit down maybe.

This was just routine. I couldn't see any profit to be made from telling them what 'a bit down' entailed.

—The phone records show that Dave Knowles called this number at 5:20. Were you at home by then?

—Yeah.

—What did he want?

I hesitated. My mind started ticking over. This was a chance. A chance to finish things.

—I never eard it ring. I must've bin crashed out. E left a message, on the machine. I only eard it this morning. Would ya like to ear it?

Course they would.

Lovely approach play ...

The pair of them couldn't make head nor tail of it. Hardly surprising. While they were being confused by the tape, I was mulling over the pros and cons. I decided to give it a whirl. It took the DS a second or two to think of a question.

—What's this mess he's on about? This mess he's got to sort out.

The ball's hanging in the air ... Falls to Andrews ...

—Last night ... Dave. How I said e were a bit down. E told me summat ... about imsen. E like came out to me.

The coppers just sat there. They'd both heard, but didn't believe it. I could tell they were waiting for me to clear up the misunderstanding.

209

—E told me that e were gay. Omosexual like.

Same reaction, only I'm sure I could see a flicker of sadistic pleasure on the fat one's dial. I backed up my claim.

—Apparently, it's bin goin on since is missus did the off.

—And he told you this last night?

Still Andrews …

—There's more. The bit about no more kids in the park. Dave said e'd picked up blokes in parks an stuff. E were too scared to go to gay bars in case e got found out. Anyway … E told me e killed a kid … in Brockwell Park. Lee summat.

YEEAASS … There it is … Andrews gave them no chance.

The detectives left about an hour later. I offered to go down the nick with them to make a statement, but they said there was no need. They weren't looking for anyone in connection with Dave's death and they'd have to make further enquiries into 'the other matter'. I wasn't going anywhere.

I collapsed on to the settee. Gradually, my heart rate returned to normal. Then it sank in. I'd pulled it off. When I was telling them about Dave's 'confession', I could see the light bulbs going on over the plods' loaves. They were stripping their image of straight up copper Dave Knowles and cooking up what was left. Take one stiff loner, add a dash of homosexuality and a traumatic marriage split. Leave to simmer. Hey presto: identikit murderer.

All the details about the killing would check out and Dave didn't have an alibi. I could tell as I went over it. They bought it. The glimmers of realisation, when things only the murderer could have known came out. Little sub-conscious nods. Being wise after the event is essential for coppers. Their old guvnor was history. They were desperate to have smelt a rat all along.

It all tied up nicely. Dave was dead. When he was alive, he'd lost everything that meant anything to him. Killer or faggot: I know which title Dave would have been more at ease with. It made no odds to him anyway. Not in his condition. There was no point in me taking a fall as well. Fucking up another family. I'm sure Dave wouldn't have wanted that.

I phoned a taxi. It was a lovely day. Suddenly, I'd got a taste for a barbecue.

European Championship Final
Germany v Czech Rep.

Sometimes, life throws up things that are impossible to predict. Example: I went through nearly thirty-two years without seeing Mick Hucknall sing, then I saw him twice in three weeks. Not on purpose either. It seemed like every time I went to a match, the cunt was in the centre circle, whining that crappy 'official' song. The fans seemed to enjoy it. Weird atmosphere it was. Seventy five per cent of Wembley was made up of England fans, who'd bought tickets in advance, hoping to be there for a historic home victory. The hosts hadn't made it; so the party was a bit flat.

It was my sixth visit to Wembley in three weeks. I'd been to all the England games and I'd been up to Old Trafford for Italy v Germany. It had changed a lot from when I'd been to England games before. Then, the crowd had been a bunch of Home Counties neo-nazis, all eager to share their considered opinions with John Barnes. The Euro 96 mob were from the other end of the spectrum entirely: couples and family groups, day trippers turning out for a spectacle. The media banged on about the 'special' atmosphere, but I thought it had gone a bit lame. Too plastic. All the 'stirring' Queen songs before the teams came out.

They'd gone overboard on the corporate hospitality as well. The number of suits at the group games had been embarrassing. That really is a case of the pot slagging off the kettle, I suppose—there's me being all righteous about it, while I survey the plebs from my free seat in the Olympic Gallery. I'd not forked out a penny at any of the matches. Well I had, but I could claim it as expenses. My suitors were picking up the tab.

GERMANY 2 CZECH REPUBLIC 1
(after sudden death extra time)

The Czechs had impressed me throughout. They had some great individuals. I'd heard whispers that a few of them would be coming over to play in the Premiership. If I was a manager, I'd have gone for the centre forward, Pavel Kuka. The lad had a lovely touch and he worked hard for the team. They had skill and quality in every department.

Germany stumbled through the championships, but they still came out on top. No one had a right to be surprised by that. Their record in major competitions is incredible. It's all down to preparation and organisation. When the stakes are high, mental toughness comes to the fore. Players need the right attitude to deal with whatever situations are thrown up. The Germans are winners: simple as that.

I couldn't really get involved in the match. In the second half, I slipped out the back to phone Jackie. I told her that I'd try to get home as quickly as possible, but she wouldn't have any of it. She said that I should enjoy the party afterwards. Stay as long as necessary. Jackie understood the importance of networking. She was really proud of me. She put Russ on the phone for a minute. My little lad Russ: only six weeks old, but he was already developing the classic good looks of his old man. He was going to break a few hearts when he got older.

The party wasn't bad at all. It was a BBC end of tournament bash. All broadcasting bods, with a smattering of name football types. In the past, I would've hated it, but not any more. That kind of do is, basically, a meat market. Full of people networking: buttering up the men at the top. Pretty sad when you're at the bottom. When you're in demand, you can sit back and get your arse kissed. My role was to smile, be myself and get courted. 5 Live were putting together a series on the history of football hooliganism. It's safe to talk about the H word these days. Despite strong evidence to the contrary, the powers that be have decided that it's no longer a problem. Time then, for a six week documentary series on fan violence. Half worthy socio-logical investigation; half sexy interviews with swaggering bad lads. The research was in place. They needed a narrator. Someone high profile. Someone respectable, but with enough street cred to speak with authority about the dodgy side. They needed Paul Andrews.

High profile? It was only a recent thing, but I was the hottest of hot properties. On the crest of the proverbial wave.

After my visit from the Laurel and Hardy plods, everything had gone quiet. I'd taken a big risk by pitching them the Dave story, but there was no action. There were a couple of weeks in limbo, then I got a strange visit. A pair of high ranking detectives came to see me, off the record. They had a cosy little chat with me.

—Not in the interests of community relations ... besmirch his memory and the reputation of the force ... retain public confidence ... best for all concerned.

They were burying the Lee Turner case. From behind a veil, they strongly advised me that I should too. That I should pretend Dave's confession never happened. I agreed to their 'suggestion'. It was, after all, what I'd been trying to do since the night in the park. As for pretending that Dave never fessed up; I managed that pretty easily.

The heat was off forever—official. The threats of shame and punishment vanished. I'd been to the edge and got away with it. I could put it behind me and get on with a normal life. For most people, that would be enough. What sets some men apart, is their ability to act under pressure. To spot an opportunity to turn a situation to their advantage.

Out of nowhere, the Lee Turner case exploded back into

life. The militant gay rights movement, Stand Out, received an anonymous letter. Its contents were dynamite.

The detective who had been in charge of the inquiry was a closet homosexual. He had murdered Lee in a frenzy of self loathing. At first, he had shielded his involvement then, unable to cope with his guilt, he had committed suicide. The Metropolitan police were aware of this and had instigated a cover up. In early April, Stand Out went public with the allegations. They named the late Detective Chief Inspector David Knowles as the Brockwell Park murderer.

The story had everything. Gay senior copper, sex, murder, cover up, sleaze. The tabloids went for it bigtime. The coppers were caught off guard. They stonewalled.

It was out. Public domain. I told Jackie everything. Correction. I told Jackie everything she needed to know about Dave's admission. We came to the same conclusion. The public had a right to know the truth.

I drove Jackie to her folks'. We decided it would be best for her to be out of the way, what with her being so far gone. When I got home, I had a belt of brandy, then dialled the number.

—Is that Rod Drummond? Alright Rod. This is Paul Andrews ...

The article came out a week later. One of Rod's chums wrote it. Very tasteful it was. That's why we picked The Guardian. We knew they'd handle it right. Three page piece in the Society section, with a tease on the front page of the paper. Nice photo of me as well.

This was the general spin of the article.

'Paul Andrews blows the lid on police cover up. He stayed silent, up to now, out of respect for the memory of his close friend, Dave Knowles. Knowles was a man who was forced to lead a double life. His gay sexuality conflicted with his high rank in an organisation which is a bastion of homophobia. This led to confusion, self disgust, the horrific murder of an innocent man and, ultimately, suicide.

'The only man he could trust enough to confide in was soccer hardman, Paul Andrews. Andrews has come forward because he is appalled by the Metropolitan Police's attempt to cover the matter up. He hopes that exposing the scandal will force the Met to address the problems of corruption and homophobia in its ranks. No longer must police officers be forced to lead double lives, like the tragic Dave Knowles.'

Has someone brought some roses in here? No. That smell must be me then. The press were fucking mad for it. I had an army of photographers camped on my doorstep.

It was time to be canny. To maximise. I got wads of offers, some of them for stupid money, but I had to be choosy. I went for the quality end. Radio Four, New Statesman profile. I could pick and choose what I fancied. There's a gay mafia in the media. Well hidden, but they're definitely there; sort of, the Puffia. They can't be totally up front, but any story with an angle will get a good hearing in the 'qualities'. All the juicy stuff got an airing in the popular press too. They couldn't knock me. Footballer, hardman, own place in Cup folklore, beautiful wife (up the stick, so he's in the clear). I came out of the story well too. Stood by my 'best' mate, even though he was one of them. Only grassed him up when the police were shown up as bent. And, of course, I solved a murder case. That lad Turner; he was a queer, but he was some mother's son.

I was a media darling. All things to all men. On the one hand, I was Paul Andrews: Yorkshire hardman, 'the lad who scored that goal against Everton that time'. Any hack who dug a bit deeper into my press cuttings would soon find some booze related ones. Most notably, an incident at a service area, which resulted in men being hospitalised and me being locked up. On the other hand, I was Paul Andrews: tolerant, concerned citizen and whistleblower. The man who spoke out to challenge injustice. A liberal man who closet gay friends can confide in. If David Batty and Graeme Le Saux had fucked each other in Moscow, instead of having a punch up, they could have given birth to my public image. Paul Andrews: a man for all seasons.

The offers came piling in as soon as the dust had settled a bit. The 5 Live thing was one of the first. The offer of free entry to Euro 96 in 'an observational capacity' made it attractive. Not only that. I think it's the right direction for me to head in.

I turned down a cable station who wanted me for a football show. I don't want to get bogged down in one area. Funnily enough, all the magazines who used to turn me down before have decided I can write after all. One of the glossies wants me to do a kind of travelogue piece on a Republic of Ireland away game. Thanks to big Mick, I'm an Eire insider these days. I even managed to flog my shitty Dublin Dons article.

And of course; there's good old South London Sound. I pretty much work when I want to down there. I'm told that old Tom's always slagging me in the boozer, but it's his own fault. He should've signed me up to a more substantial contract when he had the chance. Poor feller. I remember what it's like being a has-been. I've got better things to get on with than worrying about an old piss artist.

I left the party at two and got a cab (expenses). I always knew I was good enough. To get on you need a break. Not just that. You've got to recognise it and take it. Keep your head under pressure. I got one shot and I took it. In the circumstances, that might sound a bit callous, but it's the way of the world. There are always going to be some losers. You have sympathy for them, but not so much that it fucks up your own life. Take me and Dave. We got drawn into the same game. I dealt with it, Dave couldn't stop. I didn't fuck him over, he did it himself. Lee Turner. He was just in the wrong place at the wrong time. If you play with fire, you're going to get burnt. That night does still bother me, but I'll have to learn to live with it.

Sometimes, I drift off. Think, what would the kid be doing if he was alive? Would Dave have done it if I'd listened? Would I have made it if it hadn't happened? That's a waste of time though. If Givens had scored that penalty, Martin Peters might be England manager and I could be a redundant steelworker. If my auntie had a dick, she'd be my uncle. What's done is done. You've just got to do what's best for you and let everyone else look out for themselves.

I'm sorry they're dead, but I'm not going to spend the rest of my life on some guilt trip. As far as the record books will show, Dave Knowles murdered Lee Turner, then topped himself. After that Paul Andrews got a break in the media and went on to be successful.

End of story.

Mick Bower was born in Sheffield in 1966. At 16, he left school with one O-level. He spent the 1984/85 miners strike on a government scheme, digging ditches then filling them in again. In his late twenties Bower took A-levels and went to university, obtaining an honours degree in Politics in 1995.

Ironically, he was considered unemployable for a time after he completed his degree, and it is then (in 1995-6) that he wrote *Football Seasons*. "I got the idea for *Football Seasons* from a pub chat with an old guy I knew. After heaping praise on the Sarf London gangsters of yesteryear, he told me in graphic detail why Michael Barrymore deserved hanging. I wasn't shocked. Most lads I know would say the same. We're brought up to respect violence and hate anyone who dares to be different. It's all about fitting in. Status. Belonging to something, even if it means fuck all."